PRETTY SHATTERED MIND

ROBBI RENEE

LOVE NOTES BY RABBI RENEE

Note from the Publisher: This is a work of fiction. Any resemblance to actual persons living or dead or references to locations, persons, events, or locations is purely coincidental. The characters, circumstances and events are imaginative and not intended to reflect real events.

Pretty Shattered Mind

www.robbirenee.com

SYNOPSIS

Mind can be defined as the element of a human that gives them an awareness of the world's perspective on their experiences. The mind holds our thoughts and feelings. But what happens when the chaos of your thoughts makes it impossible to find clarity? When the noise of heart-wrenching memories drowns the whispers... the desires of your heart.

Aminah Loveless finds herself haunted by her past. Her first love, Malakai, was her one and only true love, but the scars he left behind and the promise she made him have left her wary of opening her heart again. On the surface, her life is every woman's dream: a supportive family, a blooming career, and amazing friendships, but the yearning for one key component was missing... *love.*

Nicolas Touissant was a kind-hearted and understanding man who was immediately intrigued by Aminah. Her words say she wants nothing but friendship, while their magnetic connection speaks a different language. There is no hesitation in Nicolas's heart or head. He is ready to make Aminah his one and only, give her the world.

Second-guessing her every move, Aminah finds herself torn between giving love another chance or staying committed to an unfulfilling pact. Although Nicolas's compassion and patience are potent, he is growing impatient with the pretty shattered beauty.

Nicolas and Aminah's path is fraught with challenges, uncertainty, and pain. Will their love story be a poignant exploration of friendship, adoration, and healing or will their journey end before it truly gets started?

PROLOGUE

K*ing and Syncere's Wedding - June 2021*

"Princess, I vow to always keep you safe, protect you from harm, be a shoulder to lean on when life is too much to bear on your own. I prayed for you, Syncere, and God led me to you, my wife," King declared through a quiver as he delivered his vows to Syncere.

"I praise Him today and every day as His will is being fulfilled. I will always love you, Syncere, my Princess, my love, and rejoice in your love for me, at our pace, in our time, forever."

Aminah swiped at a lone tear as her bottom lip quivered. After all that her friend, Syncere, had endured, she was so thankful that a man like King Cartwright entered her life. Watching them declare their love to one another amid an intimate gathering of family and friends was overwhelming. Aminah was flooded with an ocean of emotions as one tear turned into a soft wail.

"Well family and friends, I think we have just witnessed God's great work right before our eyes. What wonderful expressions of respect, honor, and love." Reverend Marx proceeded with the ceremony.

"I now pronounce you husband and wife. You may salute your bride."

As Luther Vandross crooned about a thousand kisses never being too much, the wedding party danced down the aisle, passing smiling guests. Nicolas clutched Aminah's hand and escorted her through the double doors, entering the space for the cocktail hour. Aminah released an exasperated breath filled with gladness and pain. Instinctively, he thumbed away a single tear traversing the curve of her cheek. He flashed a toothless smile, admiring her devastating beauty. She mimicked the gesture before quickly walking away.

The sun was tucked away behind the moon, and the wedding reception was in full swing. Aminah leaned against the balcony railing, peering out over the gorgeous vineyard. The rolling green acres appeared to go on for miles and miles. Inhaling deeply, she allowed the crisp evening air to relax her mind while the delicious wine was warming her insides. Just a couple of hours ago, her best friend, Syncere, married the love of her life, King Cartwright, with the gorgeous grounds of the winery as the backdrop.

They'd committed to a couple of forevers in an intimate ceremony surrounded by a select group of family and friends. Aminah eyed the happy couple on the dance floor, and love appeared to hover above them literally. King was attentive and in tune with his new wife's every desire. And Syncere's constant squealing, *'I'z married now,'* clearly indicated her enrapture for her husband. Aminah smiled but quickly turned away before another tsunami of tears invaded her. Roaming through the crowd, her eyes landed on one of the groomsmen who'd surprisingly been a spark of light in her darkness during the celebrative weekend.

Nicolas Touissant was a sight for sore eyes in a tan Tom Ford suit that sculpted the frame of his stocky build. He was the owner of the winery and King's best friend. The newly married couple's love story blossomed in Brighton Falls at Nic's family winery just about a year ago, so it was only fitting that they would exchange vows overlooking the gorgeous terrain.

Nicolas's stare collided with Aminah's. She flashed a delicate smile before turning to view the endless rows of grapevines softly blurred under the moon's tender glow. The sun had just dipped behind the clouds, permitting the sky to flash glimpses of sapphire and indigo.

He gazed at her, unable to withdraw his stare. Aminah appeared deep in thought, causing him to wonder what or *who* was circling through her beautiful mind. The winery's elegant silhouette was no comparison to the magnificence of Syncere's best friend and bridesmaid, Aminah Loveless. With his back pressed against the railing of the massive deck, he swiped his thumb back and forth along the rim of the whiskey glass as he got lost in the beauty of *her*.

"Her name is Aminah," King's voice rumbled behind him.

Nic snickered, then turned to face his friend.

"I know," he uttered, resuming his eye-stalking of the complicated beauty.

"Well, act like it. You're over here ogling her like you're scared."

"Nah, never that. She's just... *breathtaking*," Nic said, finally shifting to focus on King.

"What's her story?" he continued, sipping his drink. "She seems a little shy."

King pursed his lips, shrugging.

"I honestly don't know much about her. She lives in Monroe City and teaches at the university. I haven't spent a lot of time with her. For some reason, my Princess is pretty tight-lipped about Aminah. All I know is that they all met in college and have been cool ever since," King explained.

"Hmm..." Nic buzzed, turning to scan her once again.

Aminah was like a mystery to Nicolas. One he desperately wanted to solve. He'd heard about Syncere and Symphony's college friend but never met her until yesterday during the bridal party brunch. At first glance, Nicolas thought she was the most beautiful and intriguing woman he'd ever seen.

He couldn't help gawking at her ass in the short fitted dress during the rehearsal dinner last night, but today... he couldn't help but to survey how every stitch of the yellow bridesmaid's dress accentuated her brown sugar skin and hugged her shapely hips perfectly. But what *really* had Nic shook was the dewy twinkle in her copper eyes.

She's magnificent.

"I believe she's been through some shit, though," King uttered, disrupting Nic's daze.

King's assumption piqued his interest, causing him to return his attention to his friend. But he periodically checked his peripheral, ensuring she hadn't escaped his stare.

"Shit? What kind of shit?" Nic asked.

King shrugged again, taking a sip of his drink.

"Something about her ex. All I know is that shortly after me and Syncere got together, she rushed out of my place to pick up Symphony after they got an urgent call from Aminah. They drove to Monroe City and a few hours later, they brought her back to Haven. The ladies hibernated at Symphony's for a few days but that's all that I know."

A moment of silence lingered between them.

"Primo," a voice sang from behind the handsome gentlemen.

"My prima... *Your Princess* is looking for her husband," Symphony screeched, advancing towards Nicolas and King.

King's wide smile was automatically swoon-worthy.

"That's my queue, Dawg. I'll catch you later," King said, exchanging a choreographed handshake with Nic.

The hush resumed other than the faint whisper of the wind. Instinctively, Nic's eyes searched for Aminah. Symphony followed Nicolas's sightline that led her gaze right to her friend.

"Be careful with her, Nic," Symphony said sternly.

Snickering, his eyes shifted away from one complicated beauty just to regard another.

"And what does that mean, Symphony? Why are you telling me that?"

Momentarily, Symphony's gray orbs shifted to observe Aminah, too.

"Earth, wind, and fire," she whimpered.

Nic was voiceless but the crease in his forehead indicated confusion.

"Me, Syncere, and Aminah. Of course I'm the fire," she chuckled before continuing.

"Syncere is our earth and Minah..." Symphony paused, shaking her head with a slight smile curving her lips.

"She's the wind. Fragile and free, yet, a chaotic energy ready to wreak havoc at any moment."

Nicolas lightly chuckled, not fully comprehending Symphony's words but digesting them, nonetheless.

"Aminah has lost a lot, Nic, but refuses to grieve. So it's just a matter of time before she breaks. Just be careful," Symphony declared, lifting her wine glass, seemingly seeking his understanding.

Nicolas obliged, connecting the rim of his glass with hers.

Abruptly, Symphony was swept away by another groomsman, Tyus Okoro. She giggled and Nic shook his head.

Gulping down the last sip of brown liquor, he placed the glass on a tray held by a passing server. Clearing his throat, he strolled across the room to acquaint himself with *her.*

The sparkling lights stretched across the deck, reflected in her pretty eyes. Nicolas recognized specks of joy, warmth, and sadness in the core of her copper orbs. Music and laughter wafted through a gentle breeze, rustling the tresses of her bone-straight hair.

"Hello, Beautiful," he muttered from behind her.

Aminah slowly spun around with a sweet blush painting her pretty face.

"I don't believe we've been formally introduced," he continued teasingly.

"Hi, Nicolas," she sang.

"Nic. My friends call me Nic."

"Hi, Nic." The rasp of her voice was the sweetest song.

Sliding his teeth across his smooth bottom lip, he licked it before uttering, "Hi, Love."

Twelve Months Before the Cartwright Wedding

"Malakai," Aminah groaned questioningly, being jolted from her slumber.

The soft knocking noise that awakened her paused momentarily and then restarted with a bit more bass. With barely one eye opened, she glanced at the clock on the nightstand.

2am.

Stretching her arm across the bed, she grumbled again, "Malakai."

But he was not in the bed.

Boom!

Aminah shot up and scrambled out of the bed to identify the location of the commotion. Her eyes frantically darted around the room in search of the culprit. Snatching her phone, she slid out of the bed and tip-toed to the dresser to grab the crystal vase from the dresser. Peeking down the dim hallway, she continued to creep toward the light coming from downstairs. She calmed slightly once she heard the bass of the reggae beat. Malakai.

Lately, he'd awake at all hours of the night with what he called *inspiration* to paint. What he considered inspiration, Aminah deemed just plain annoying. Peering over the railing into the great room of her two-story townhouse, she recognized his silhouette.

Eyeing the vase, she chuckled before placing the heavy crystal on a nearby table and then scaling the stairs. Dressed in boy shorts and a tank top, she shivered a little once her bare feet touched the cool hardwood floor.

Outside, it was a warm summer day, but inside, it felt like Antarctica. Rubbing her hands up and down her arms, she crossed the great room to look at the thermostat. *Sixty-one degrees. What the hell?*

"Kai, baby, it's freezing in here," she uttered, entering the sunroom that doubled as his studio.

The corner of her mouth turned into a lustful smile, and her eyes were wide at the sight of him. He was shirtless, exposing smooth butter pecan skin with gray sweatpants sitting low on his waist. Wispy hair peaked above the elastic band, but it was the bulge stretching the cotton fabric that she couldn't snatch her eyes from. His shoulder-length locs were pulled into a loose man-bun at the crown of his head. Malakai was beautiful.

When Aminah met him on the campus of Monroe University as a shy freshman, she was initially intimidated by the gorgeous creature who was a delicious combination of Bob Marley and Lenny Kravitz. Malakai Winston was an eclectic, artistic spirit who was in no hurry to finish his education. He graduated from Monroe after six years and then took a few years to travel the world before returning to the university as a graduate student in the art school.

Malakai was a teaching assistant when he first saw Aminah sitting expectantly in the front row of his art history class. The young and naive beauty was oblivious to his advances because he was charismatic and a little flirtatious with all of the girls. The verbal sparring over his class's front row seats was comical. But Malakai only had eyes for one student.

Five years her senior, he kept his distance for almost two years until late one Thursday afternoon when she walked into his office to apply for a tutoring position. The on-the-spot interview turned into dinner at the local pub then four years of Malakai and Aminah's love story.

They were two peas in a pod. Inseparable and madly in love. Aminah graduated with her bachelor's degree and was finishing the last semester of her graduate program. At the same time, Malakai was a full-time artist and part-time director of the university's art museum. The beautiful diamond ring sparkling on her dainty finger indicated their next step towards happily ever after.

"Kai, come back to bed, babe. It's late... or early," Aminah said, rubbing her eyes as she yawned.

Malakai remained hushed but his body jerked almost uncontrollably. Squinting through tired, reddened eyes, Aminah actually looked at him for the first time since entering the room. He appeared to be in another world. Incomprehensible mumbles fell from his mouth. The same jumbled words were repeated as he erratically stroked the paintbrush on the canvas. His locs escaped from the elastic holder, wildly swaying with each frantic movement.

"Kai... Baby, are you ok?" Aminah asked, slowly... hesitantly closing the distance between them.

"I have to finish this, Peanut. This could be my next masterpiece," he exclaimed through staggered breaths, never making eye contact with her.

Aminah rounded the easel holding the oversized canvas and gasped. Darting her eyes back and forth from the painting to him, she was speechless. The image of a gruesome, devilish creature with horrifying, blood red eyes was staring back at her.

"Malakai. What is this?" she stammered.

"It's my best work. Right, Peanut?"

She shook her head, unable to formulate a sentence. This was not his best work. Malakai was popular for his ability to make the most simple scenes into stunning visuals. His eyes captured things the rest of the world could not see. The most captivating portraits of everyday people simply thriving in their elements. Many of his masterpieces decorated the halls of Monroe University and the homes of his many esteemed clients.

But lately, Malakai's work was different... dark. *He'd* been different. Isolated, confused, and belligerent at times. He'd missed a few critical deadlines at work and that behavior was unlike him.

Nights filled with insomnia, turned to days of hibernation. But most recently, Malakai had become anxious and aggressive. Anything could trigger him to lash out. He was not an imposing figure physically, but Malakai's presence always bordered on intimidation... demanding attention by any means necessary. And given his recent behavior, caution and fear cloaked Aminah's demeanor.

"Kai, baby, come to bed. You need to get some rest," Aminah muttered.

She gently touched his shoulder, and he jerked, eyeing her dangerously. His eyes were bulging and glossy.

"You're just like them," he said, grunting.

"Like who?" Aminah whispered.

"Like Dean Logan, my clients, my family. You don't understand my art. You want me to keep doing the same old shit," he spat.

"Kai, baby. I do understand. You're a magnificent artist. I just think you just need some rest. Please, come back to bed." Aminah reached out to touch him when he jerked away angrily.

Flailing his arm, he knocked over the canvas and cans, causing paint to splatter everywhere.

"Malakai..." Aminah shrieked as she jumped back to avoid the mess.

He quickly closed the distance between them, forcing her trembling body against the wall.

"I heard the shit you've been saying. You think I'm crazy. Like I've lost my fucking mind. I'm not crazy, Aminah. *I'm not fucking crazy*," he screamed as spit dotted her face.

"Kai. Baby. I don't think you're crazy."

"No," he said questioningly. "Then what the fuck is this?" he inquired, snatching a piece of paper from a table a few steps across the room.

Aminah hurriedly lifted from the wall and slowly moved towards the house phone in the kitchen. Malakai followed her.

"Look at this shit. They're firing me."

Aminah's head cocked back.

"What? You got fired?"

She intently read the paperwork dated over a week ago.

. . .

Malakai Winston,

Your termination is effective immediately. You have two hours to retrieve any personal belongings and security will escort you from the premises.

Dean Logan

"Kai. What happened? Why would they need security? What is going on?"

"So, this is my fault? You're blaming *me* for their bullshit."

"No. No, baby. I'm not blaming you. I just want to understand what's going on. Malakai. Maybe we should talk to the doctor again. Kai, I - I want to help you." A trail of tears soaked her cheeks.

In an abrupt move, he hopped onto the countertop, causing her to shudder. An eerie calm came over him. Through flushed, squinted eyes, he leered at her. Disdain and lunacy darkened his eyes.

"I need help because I'm crazy, Peanut," Malakai said, his tone throaty.

Aminah had been walking on eggshells for six months in her own home. Unsure of what or who could trigger his madness. They'd visited therapists and doctors who all prescribed medication but he refused to take it.

That shit fucks with my creative process, Peanut. Malakai would complain.

Typically, the loving nickname he marked her with years ago meant that his rage-filled episode was tempering. But the knife he retrieved from the block on the counter signaled that his eruption was just getting started.

Malakai pricked the skin of his forearm over and over while blankly staring at Aminah. Shit, *through her.* Blood bubbled then rolled down his arm, but he wasn't fazed.

"Kai, don't do this, please. Please," she begged, snapping her fingers in a desperate attempt to end his haze.

"Can you see me, Kai? It's me. Minah. Your Peanut. Please put the knife down."

Miraculously, Aminah appeared composed, but terror thundered through her core. She swallowed the boulder to quell the adrenaline pulsing through her veins. Her eyes flickered with fierce intensity as she fought to maintain control in the chaotic scene unfolding before her.

Unexpectedly, he jumped off of the counter and lunged for her. With the knife still in his hand, he pressed her petite body against the kitchen island. As his hand tightened around her neck, so did her fear. Their frantic breaths harmoniously quickened.

Aminah eyed the tip of the shiny metal dangling in her face. She held her breath, afraid that any movement would cause him to snap. Malakai flattened the knife and traced it across her skin. Aminah's chest quaked with the need to breathe. Each painful exhale was a silent plea. A puddle of tears blurred her vision, leaking on to the knife.

"Kai," she croaked under the pressure of his hold on her neck.

Malakai jumped, piercing her chin. Aminah screamed, not from pain, but the shock of his behavior. Recognition immediately covered him like quicksand. He stepped back, dropping the knife on the floor. She breathed a sigh of relief when his delirium slowly diminished, but the reprieve was only momentary.

Raising his hand to her face, Aminah shoved him away, snatching the cordless phone during her escape. She dashed up the stairs but quickly realized that he was not following. The creak of the garage door opening could always be heard from the second floor. The engine of the Mustang she despised roared to life. The powerful hum vibrated the whole house.

Aminah rushed to the window in the loft just in time to see Malakai speed away wildly.

Boom!

"Malakai! Nooo!"

1

PRESENT DAY

"Shit!"

Aminah jolted from the memory, dropping the glass coffee mug, shattering it against the deep walnut tiled floor in the kitchen.

"*Be careful, Peanut.*"

Echoes of his gruff morning timbre echoed through her psyche. She closed her eyes, imagining the swipe of his knuckle down her cheek, creating an instant calm when she was frazzled.

"Lord, I think I'm going crazy," she mumbled to no one but herself.

Aminah shook her head, nervously panning through the kitchen to clean up her mess. Visions of Malakai had been so vivid lately. She could hear and see him as if his chocolate stocky frame was standing before her. But that was impossible - her love, her dream, her fiancé was gone.

It had been months since she envisioned him in that way. Dreams of him were becoming more infrequent over the years, but when they surfaced, he penetrated every thread of her core. Haunting and pervading, his presence persisted throughout that day. Aminah could smell his cologne, feel the coarseness of his locs between her fingertips, and taste remnants of his favorite bourbon dancing on her lips.

Three years. It had been years since Malakai left and Aminah still found herself questioning God. Her parents and friends urged, practically begged her, to move forward. To find peace and happiness in something other than her work.

Aminah Loveless was an art history professor at her alma mater, Monroe University. Since the heartbreaking change in her life, she constantly filled her days with a full course load of classes and extracurricular activities. Burying herself in work was an understatement. Aminah was trying to escape the frantic, insomnia filled nights, but there was no remedy. At least not until the last couple of years. *Not until Nic.*

Aminah glanced at the digital microwave clock. *Maybe I shouldn't go. Kai won't let go today. He's going to linger.* She mused silently, almost hearing him whisper, *"You damn right, Peanut."*

Aminah shook her head, adjusting the red robe that draped her curvy frame. Aimlessly meandering to her bedroom, she opened the French doors to the gorgeous black and white bathroom and tiptoed across the tiled floor into the closet. Aminah placed a fingertip to her chin, fondling the tiny, but noticeable scar on her chin.

The massive closet offered too many clothing options to consider for a day at the winery. She disrobed, laying the plush fabric across the ottoman centered in the room while staring at herself in the floor to ceiling mirror.

Monochromatic hued eyes a shade lighter than her skin stared back at her. Others saw strength, endurance, and resilience in those eyes. Aminah saw nothing but fear, anxiety, and sorrow. But today she saw a glimpse of something different - hope and excitement. A new vision momentarily invaded her mind because of *him.*

Skin the color of clay, tawny orbs, and a pleasantly imposing thickset frame caused the corner of her pouty lips to rise.

"Is that a smile Aminah Rae?" her mother blurted, standing in the threshold of the closet.

Aminah was the spitting image of Desirae Loveless. The identical face was aged to perfection at fifty-seven years old with subtle streaks of gray hair.

"Mommy! Oh my goodness. You scared me. And I'm naked."

Aminah snatched her robe, hurriedly covering herself.

"Girl please. I wiped your ass. You don't have anything I ain't seen. You don't have anything I ain't got," her mother chuckled, slapping against her curvy hips that she shared with her daughter.

"Did you decide what you're going to wear?" Mrs. Loveless asked.

Aminah was about to speak but her mother continued.

"I would wear the coral dress. That looks amazing against your skin. Nic is already wowed by you, but that dress will make him fall to his knees and beg you to never leave." Desirae dramatically clasped her hands.

"That is not the goal, Mommy. I'm just going to hang out with Nic for the day. And besides, we're just friends. I'm not looking-"

"I know. I know. You're not looking for anything serious."

Since meeting at King and Syncere's wedding, Nic had been enamored with the beautiful Aminah Rae Loveless. She was a tiny little thing who despised being called *petite* because in her words, *"My presence is tall."*

Aminah gained a few inches when she flexed her red-bottom

stilettos, but on any other day, she was about three, maybe four inches over five feet. But the thickness that was attached to that body was undeniable.

Velvety smooth skin the color of maple syrup sheathed the perfect C cup teardrop breasts. A fairly taut waist, thanks to years of dance and gymnastics, and perfectly crafted hips bordering that apple of an ass.

What started as cute flirtation between the two quickly morphed into a friendship sprinkled with growing adoration. At least for Nic. He more than adored Aminah; he loved her. Nic never masked his feelings nor intentions for his lovie, but she kept him locked in the friend zone.

While she was potentially open to a *benefriends* situation, Nicolas wasn't game at all. He wanted to skip all of the formalities and make her Mrs. Touissant. But as much as her body craved him and her heart wanted to love him, her mind could not... would not open up to Nic.

I promised Kai. Aminah often pondered.

Her mother rolled her eyes in response to the *just friends* comment. Mrs. Loveless stepped behind her daughter, gazing at their similar reflections in the mirror.

"Minah, Nic wants more than a friendship, honey. You have been using this 'just friends' excuse for years," she motioned air quotes.

"So you have to be honest with him about what you're capable of giving *and* receiving. I love Malakai like my own son and miss what you two had, but he would want you to be happy, Aminah Rae. You hear me?"

Aminah nodded, but she wasn't convinced. She wouldn't tell her mother about the dreams. About her promise. Couldn't utter a word about feeling haunted by Malakai.

"Promise me, Aminah. You'll never love another, right Peanut?" The slow rhythm of the hospital machines boomed.

"Right." She pondered her response from all those years ago.

Aminah shook her head to snap out of her reverie.

"Um, how long are you all staying, Ma?" Aminah endeavored to change the subject.

Mrs. Loveless rolled her eyes.

"You kicking us out," her mother teased.

Aminah shook her head.

Her parents had been visiting Monroe City for several days to check on their rental properties but it was just an excuse to check on her.

"I'm just asking because I may be in Haven next week. Actually, I may be there for a few weeks to explore the Executive Director position for the university's new foundation," Aminah announced.

"Minah! Are you moving back home?" her mother squealed.

"Slow your roll, Lady Loveless. I'm *thinking* about if the job is right for me. You know I have a few offers on the table but I haven't made any decisions yet," she clarified before her mother started planning weekly brunch dates.

"Is one of those offers London?" her mother asked, scowling.

Aminah nodded.

"Yes and no. London is a short-term opportunity that *may* have long-term potential. They've offered me the opportunity to teach a summer intensive and interview in-person. I haven't been offered anything yet."

"Well, you know, Daddy and I would love for you to be closer to home. But I just want you to be happy, Mi. And if London is the answer, then I say go for it." Her mother cupped her chin and kissed her on the nose.

Aminah smiled because her parents always supported her in every endeavor, whether or not they agreed with the decision.

"What does Nic think?" Mrs. Loveless continued to probe.

Aminah said nothing, busying herself by pretending to shuffle through the closet.

"Aminah Rae," her mother said sternly.

She rolled her eyes, knowing that her mother meant business when she added *Rae* to her name.

"We haven't talked about it," Aminah muttered.

"You haven't talked about it because you haven't told that man," Desirae fussed.

Aminah shook her head and so did her mother.

"I'm going to say this and then I'm done with it," she said, pausing momentarily to wait for her daughter to look at her.

Begrudgingly, Aminah lifted her eyes to her mother.

"If Nic is truly your friend like you claim, he'll support you in whatever you decide. But if you do not tell him..." Desirae shook her head. "Be prepared to lose a good friend... And a good man."

Aminah swallowed hard while nodding.

"But you're a grown woman and whatever decision you make, you stand by it, you hear me?" Desirae declared.

Aminah nodded, while whispering, "I hear you, Ma."

"I think a change of scenery will be cleansing for you, honey. "

Aminah rested her head on her mother's shoulder before releasing a deep sigh.

"Yeah, me too."

She'd considered moving at least a dozen times but loved working for the university. Monroe City had many positive memories, but she wanted to permanently erase some. She delivered a loud smooch against her mother's cheek. Glancing at the clock again, Aminah hurried to the bathroom.

"So the coral dress, huh," she said, lifting a brow seeking approval from her mother.

Desirae nodded with a smile. Aminah smiled, too, gently pushing her mother out of the closet.

"Scoot, Lady Loveless. Let me get dressed. Nic is a stickler for time."

"Mm-hmm. I bet he'd be a *stickler* for something else too," her mother teased.

"Ma," Aminah squealed through a chuckle as her mother shuffled out of the room.

2

The oversized iron gate with a 'T' scripted in the center on each side opened as she turned onto the narrow road. Touissant Winery was one of the most beautiful pieces of land in Brighton Falls. The forty-five minute drive from Monroe City was relaxing, but Aminah's nerves were suddenly shot.

Nic and Aminah had spent time together in the past since they'd met at the wedding of their best friends, King and Syncere. But lately their dynamic was different. *She* was different. The friendly feelings she had for Nic were quickly morphing into something else. *Something* that caused a rush of warmth cascading through her pussy. The delicate kisses to her temple, the way he called her *Lovie,* simmered a small flame that grew more fierce, more intense with every brush of his fingertips.

Aminah's left leg trembled as she continued her journey down the slender path. It expanded, leading her past the bed and breakfast house, and the main building with the cafe, event space, and tasting room.

Pulling her red Mercedes GLE Coupe into the driveway of the immaculate home, she inhaled deeply, gathering herself before being in his presence. The more time she spent with Nic, the harder it became to tame the beast rumbling in her center. As much as she hated to admit it, Aminah wanted to experience him... *everywhere.*

The clang of the oversized door opening disrupted her ponder. Aminah smiled because there he was. A whole order of all man, with a side of extra fine.

Excitedly, she opened her door, stepped out of the car, and immediately cringed. Nic shook his head, ready to chastise her for disregarding his attempt to be chivalrous. Closing the door she mouthed, *sorry,* as he chuckled.

Nic lazily strolled down the steps, his hands stuffed in his pocket. He smiled the sexiest, panty-wetting smile. Haunting voices and visuals often ceased in his presence. Nic was simply beautiful.

Aminah eyed the sleeve tattoo that peeked out of the top of his t-shirt and snaked down his entire right arm. The tattoo pattern resumed to the lower half of his left leg. She wondered if Nic had other ink that was not visible to the naked eye.

"Good morning, gorgeous," Nicolas greeted.

He wrapped a firm hand around her nape, planting his lips against the piercing on the fatty part of her ear. Nic found the oddest ways to express his adoration but Aminah wasn't complaining. The simplicity of his touch was enough to calm her anxiety, but at the same time, it caused a commotion. This man was just way too sexy for it to be so early in the damn morning.

"Good morning, Nic. Am I late?" Aminah scrunched her button nose as she often did when nervous and unsure.

"No, you're right on time, Love. Come here." He crooked his finger, beckoning her to him.

Aminah practically floated to the man. Nic needed her to be closer; in that moment, Aminah realized she needed him near, too. Due to their travel schedules, they hadn't seen each other in a couple of weeks. Text message exchanges and video calls were not enough for Nic. He missed her. The invitation to brunch was his opportunity to have Aminah all to himself.

Drawing her into a firm yet gentle hug, he kissed her temple, then uttered, "I missed you, Lovie."

Aminah blushed. Whenever he called her *love* or *lovie,* it was like a new day. Nic never planned for the moniker to stick, it was just instinct... *Shit,* appropriate. Aminah Rae Loveless *was* his love.

The first time they met, there was instant attraction—an immediate friendship. Aminah vainly attempted to dismiss what she was feeling for Nic because her loss was still fresh, but he kept coming around—being what she didn't even know she needed. Nic was patient. He paid attention to every detail and listened when she had everything and nothing to say.

Nic wasn't free of loss either when they met. He was grieving his father's death and the end of a long-term relationship so his defenses were high as well. The timing was all wrong but he couldn't deny the pull. Aminah tugged at his heartstrings no matter how inconvenient it may have been.

A friendship was the agreement because it was better than nothing at all. Countless nights video chatting turned into weekend visits to Monroe City or road trips to Haven Pointe. Sleepless nights that plagued her for years were erased when wrapped in Nic's arms. Their connection wasn't intimate, it was... respite, for them both.

Nonetheless, they'd become an integral part of each other's

life. Aminah lived in every fabric of his being, while Nic provoked a level of peace that she hadn't experienced in years. All she had to do was say the word and Nic would oblige her every need. But unfortunately, the mind did not always allow room for what the heart desired.

Reluctantly releasing her from his hold, Nic took a few steps back to absorb the stunning beauty that stood before him. Aminah followed her mother's advice by wearing the coral dress and draping her faux locs into a high ponytail. Her parents had been married for thirty years so she figured Desirae Loveless knew *a little* something about impressing a man.

But you're not trying to impress him, remember? You're just friends.

Lies, she thought.

"You're a fucking vision, Love," Nic blurted and Aminah blushed.

"How'd your trip end?" she asked, accepting his outstretched hand.

"It was productive," Nic declared nonchalantly.

"And yours?" he probed.

"Productive," she giggled.

Nic nodded then motioned his head toward the house.

"Come on. Breakfast is ready."

He ushered her up the steps and across the threshold of his family's home.

"Oh my goodness. Your home is beautiful, Nic." She peered around digesting the mixture of antique fixtures and modern decor.

"Why didn't we get the grand tour during the wedding weekend?"

"Renovations," he said. "But, thank you. There's a lot of memories in this house."

She nodded, circling her eyes in admiration of the architectural design.

"Are you hungry? The food is ready but if you'd prefer a tour of the house first..." he questioned but was quickly cut off.

"I'm starved. Let's eat," Aminah chuckled.

"Right this way, Ms. Loveless."

He motioned, directing her towards the kitchen.

Photos of the Touissant family painted the walls leading to the kitchen. His father, his mother, him, and his younger sister appeared to be the perfect black family dressed alike in the holiday portrait. They continued through the expansive gourmet kitchen then entered the closed patio overlooking the beautifully manicured backyard.

Aminah aimlessly meandered through the space surveying her surroundings, noticing the eggs, bacon, and assortment of pastries, breads, and fruit plated on the sideboard.

"Did you cook all of this, Nic?" Her eyes darted across the spread of food.

"I wish I could take the credit for this, but no. My sister, Chef Naomi, prepares meals for the bed and breakfast guests so I made a few special requests just for you."

He winked.

"Oh that's right. Her food was delicious at the wedding. Has she always been the winery's chef?" Aminah questioned, selecting a juice to make a mimosa.

"No, just for the past five years or so. Naomi can cook just about anything but she's famous for her maple syrup cinnamon rolls."

Aminah's eyes ballooned.

"My teeth are aching just thinking about it, but I can't leave here without indulging," she quipped.

"Most definitely. I got you, Love."

He winked again and she melted a little.

Nicolas disappeared into the house while Aminah walked around the patio admiring the perennials that filled the space. Sipping a pineapple mimosa from the champagne flute, she gazed out of the floor to ceiling sliding door, admiring the beautiful rose garden.

"A yellow rose for my yellow rose."

A voice whispered in her psyche. She closed her eyes, recalling the fresh aroma of the roses. Aminah's body lightly jerked, unsure if she was intrigued by the memory or frightened.

Malakai snuggled behind Aminah, kissing against her neck when he revealed a single yellow rose.

"Kai, you scared me. What are you doing here, Bae?" Aminah beamed, peering around the university library to ensure her manager wasn't watching.

"I needed to hear you say you love me, Peanut."

"You know I love you, Kai."

"You promise to love me and only me? Forever?" Malakai persisted.

"You can dig in if you're ready," Nic's baritone resounded.

Aminah jolted, blinking rapidly to clear her haze.

"I'm sorry. I didn't mean to startle you. Are you ok?"

Nicolas eyed her curiously from the entryway. She nodded, offering him a slight smile.

He entered the room carrying a serving tray with two coffee cups, a coffee pot, and all the fixings. Setting it on the table, Nic strolled towards her then lifted his hand to cup her chin.

"Are you sure you're good?"

Aminah mildly quivered, attempting to shake the memory. Malakai would enter her psyche at the most inopportune times. The smallest things could trigger a memory. Today it was roses.

In the past, the recollections invaded her daily; always concluding with, *'promise to love me and only me? Forever?'*

She nodded, declaring, "Yes, Nic. I'm good. Let's eat," she snickered nervously.

He gazed for a second longer, deciding not to press her. Clasping her hand, he guided them to the table and pulled out a chair for her to be seated.

"I don't think you're as complicated as Syncere when it comes to your coffee," he chuckled. "If I remember correctly, just almond milk and two sugars, right?"

"Right," Aminah cosigned.

The blush heating her cheeks could not be prevented. She adored that he was so attentive to her. Nicolas fixed her plate with eggs, bacon, sausage, and the infamous maple syrup cinnamon roll.

"This looks delicious. Thank you, Nic."

He nodded.

They ate in silence for a long minute. Aminah scooped a fork full of the cinnamon roll and audibly groaned.

"Oh my god. This thing is - oh my goodness."

She continued to stuff her face full of the warm, sticky pastry.

"It's the shit, right?" he laughed, leaning back in his chair.

"The cafe opens at seven, and these are gone by nine o'clock every morning. Naomi only offers them on the weekends. I've met people who drove up to Brighton the night before from St. Louis and Kansas City just to be in line the next morning for these things," Nic laughed.

"Well, give the chef my regards. They are *magnifique*." Aminah kissed her fingers.

"Give them yourself," Nicolas snickered, his eyes on the patio door.

A gorgeous, womanly version of him walked through the patio door dressed in denim skinny jeans and a white chef's jacket with the Touissant logo on the left side and *Chef Naomi* embroidered on the right. Her short cut, blonde, curly coils framed her pretty face.

"Good morning, Nicky," Naomi smiled brightly at the sight of her brother.

The sibling connection was apparent.

"Good morning, Nomi," Nic returned her salutation.

"This is my friend, Aminah Loveless. Lovie, this is my beautiful and annoying little sister, Naomi. Or as she's affectionately called in our family, Nomi."

"Hi, Aminah. It is nice to finally meet you. I remember you from King's wedding but I don't believe we met." Naomi extended her hand to Aminah.

"Nice to meet you as well, Naomi. Breakfast was amazing. Girl, those cinnamon rolls...whew! I may need to take a few for my parents. My father would love them," Aminah chirped.

"Consider it done. I'll make sure someone brings you some from the cafe before you leave," she offered, smiling.

"I didn't mean to disrupt your breakfast, I just needed to get something from my room," Naomi announced.

"When do you head out, Nomi?" Nicolas asked, taking the last bite of his cinnamon roll.

"I'm going to leave around three. My flight leaves tonight at eight-twenty but I want to go by Mommy's house first."

Aminah's eyes pranced between Nic and his sister, admiring their loving exchange.

"Nomi's headed to Aruba," Nic announced.

"Yep, with my boo," Naomi squealed and Nic rolled his eyes.

"Whatever, Nicky. Amir is cool. You just need to get to know him."

Nicolas's nod wasn't convincing.

"It was nice meeting you, Aminah. It's going to be a beautiful day so you two have fun." Naomi closed the distance between her and Nic, pulling him into a hug.

"Nadine is covering the cafe so you have nothing to worry about. I will see you next Wednesday. Love you, brother," she declared.

Nic kissed against her forehead.

"I love you more. Be careful, Nomi. I'm serious."

"I know, I know. I have all the best birth control," Naomi teased, as she trotted out of the room, avoiding her brother's fiery gawk.

Aminah freed an endearing giggle.

"Y'all are too cute."

"Do you have any siblings?" Nic inquired.

"I'm technically an only child, but my parents raised my cousin so he's like my little brother," Aminah explained.

"Yeah, she drives me crazy but that's my baby girl. We're only eighteen months apart but she's still my baby sister," Nic teased.

Aminah smirked adoringly, admiring his adoration for his sister.

"That's sweet."

She couldn't tame the lust-laced grin painting her face.

Naomi bid them farewell once again before navigating through the kitchen and out of sight. They sat in silence but it wasn't awkward. It was... meditative. Nic gazed at her and she regarded him.

"You ready for a tour?" he asked.

The gleam brightening her face couldn't be denied as she nodded. Nic extended his hand for her to follow him. They meandered down a long hallway as he pointed out the vintage features of the home.

"This place is magnificent, Nic. How did a black family become owners of a winery? In Missouri, nonetheless," Aminah questioned as Nic gave her a tour of the five bedroom, four bath house.

"I get confused with all of the greats, but I think it was my paternal great, great, great grandparents who fled the south and became free slaves. The Touissant family owned the land but it was a farm. They would house freed slaves as long as they worked the land. My family and others lived in what is now the bed and breakfast house. I'm not really sure how the Touissant family came here from France but their olive skin didn't make them very popular with the white folks in town so they created a little village."

Nic lifted his eyebrows seeking Aminah's understanding.

"The owner, Mr. Touissant, fell in love with my great great grandmother and they had four children. The details get a little lost because the owner Touissant suddenly died shortly after they transitioned the land to become a vineyard. The family lost the land for a while until my great grandfather bought it back in the 1940s. And the rest is history. My grandfather, Nicolas Touissant, made the place a staple in Brighton Falls. Then my father, Nicolas Touissant, Jr., and now me - Nicolas Touissant, the third," he chuckled and Aminah joined the boisterous laughter.

"That's an amazing story, Nic. I would love to research that more. There's great artistic history that lives between the lost details that I would love to uncover."

Aminah beamed at the thought.

"Be my guest. I would love that. There's a ton of old pictures in the attic of the bed and breakfast and this house that we never had the energy to sort through."

"So basically you could be sitting on my tenure at the university," she said teasingly.

He chuckled, "Maybe."

Nic and Aminah perched on the porch swing for hours discussing his family's history, her family, school, everything and nothing at the same time. Nic was her peace, a sense of serenity. It was just so easy with him.

With Malakai, he always needed attention, required constant validation and assurance. Nic, on the other hand, was assured, quiet in the midst of her mental storm. And that shit was scary - because the memories of Malakai took a temporary hiatus only amid Nicolas's calm.

"Ok, Professor Loveless, your turn," Nic exclaimed.

Aminah rapidly blinked, returning her attention to the conversation.

"You told me when you fell in love with art, you said poetry was actually your creative outlet. What's your favorite poem?" Nic sexily smirked as they began to leisurely stroll the winery grounds.

Aminah softly smiled, reminiscing on the last time she recited this poem.

Malakai.

"What happens to a dream deferred? Does it dry up like a raisin in the sun? Or fester like a sore– And then run? Does -" Aminah stuttered, eyes widened when Nic joined her.

They simultaneously recited.

"Does it stink like rotten meat? Or crust and sugar over– like a syrupy sweet? Maybe it just sags like a heavy load. Or does it explode?"

Nic and Aminah shared matching beams as they flawlessly uttered the words as if they were meant to be.

He laughed, plucking a flower from the rose bush, placing it in her hair. Nic motioned so effortlessly, stroking a finger down the arc of her face, resting at the scar on her chin.

"Langston Hughes," Nic blurted.

She nodded.

"I was assigned that poem for the eighth grade Black History Month program. So damn embarrassing." He shook his head.

"I bet you were so handsome in your Sunday best outfit for the program," Aminah giggled.

"Yeah, my moms made me wear a tie *and* goofy ass shoes," he laughed.

"I was introduced to Langston Hughes in the eighth grade, too. Language arts class. Ms. Gilford was my favorite teacher. She was 'woman three in beauty salon' in Poetic Justice ya know." Aminah lifted a reassuring brow as if her favorite teacher was Janet Jackson.

Nicolas couldn't prevent his snicker. She pushed his brawny arm but he didn't budge.

"Seriously, Nic. Ms. Gilford was a superstar to me. She not only introduced me to poetry...she made me understand the beauty and genius of black writers like Nikki Giovanni, Audre Lorde, and even Paul Laurence Dunbar. Cynthia Gilford taught me countless lessons that I remember to this day. I can hear her saying, '*Aminah darling, if you don't use your craft, you may as well just lay down and die*'."

Aminah laughed at the memory, sipping her favorite Touissant Winery Red Blend.

"Where is the infamous Ms. Cynthia Gilford now?" Nicolas inquired, clutching her hand to aid in navigating a steep hill.

"I don't know. She has to be well into her sixties now. But I'm sure she's still impacting the lives of shy, self-conscious little black girls." Aminah dreamily peered out into the setting sun overlooking the glorious winery grounds.

Nicolas couldn't get enough of her. Syrup-hued eyes that appeared basic to the naked eye, but for him, they mirrored the perfection of a rare jasper stone. He stared. Ogled her with no words.

"Is running your family's winery what you always wanted to do?" Aminah asked, motioning her finger to illustrate the winery's acreage expanse.

He shuddered. Her sweet voice pleasantly interrupted his reverie, but he remained hushed.

"Oh. I'm sorry if that question was too personal." She coyly shrugged.

"No." Nic lightly chuckled. "That's not it at all. Lovie, you can ask me anything. It's just that...no one has ever asked me what I wanted."

Nic intertwined his pinky finger with hers as they continued to slowly meander.

"What do you mean?" she probed.

"My parents were so focused on maintaining the family legacy, they kinda forgot about asking me and my sister what we wanted. I vowed to get as far away from this place as possible - hence joining the AirForce."

"Growing up in a small town like Brighton, you dream about exploring the world. Shit, when we visited family in St. Louis, me and Naomi thought that was the biggest city ever."

They simultaneously laughed.

"But after the military and college, I wanted to live...everywhere. I did a few years in New York, a few in LA, and even a stint in London."

"And what brought you back to beautiful Brighton?" Aminah continued to investigate.

Nic halted for a long moment.

"My father," he whimpered.

"Pressure to take over the family business, huh?" she probed.

"Nah. I'm sure that's what he wanted, but he was happy for me. Dad wanted me to live the life I thought was best. But I'm sure he secretly wished that his only son - his namesake - would run the family business. But... he died."

Nicolas deeply inhaled then audibly released a painful sigh. His beautiful hickory orbs fixed on the darkening landscape as nightfall traded places with the sun.

"Right here on the land that he cherished, doing the very thing that he loved. Five years ago, Dad woke up before the sun like any other day, readying himself to join the maintenance team as he often did. He had a massive heart attack shortly after they arrived. He was in his favorite place, the heart of the vineyard."

Nicolas rubbed a hand down his face to quell the emotions invading his spirit.

"Nic. I - I'm so sorry. I didn't mean to pry."

Aminah knew that his father died but she never asked about the circumstances. She gently pressed a hand to his chest, pausing his amble.

Nicolas's six foot height wasn't imposing, but he was a giant compared to Aminah's petite frame. He gazed down at her, lifting his hand to allow his fingertips to massage the peak of her chin. The unsuspected motion was weird and loving and sexy at the same damn time.

"You're good, Love." He assured her. "I came home because my mother and my sister needed me."

Nicolas stuffed his hands in the pockets of the shorts sexily hanging from his athletic thighs and bowed legs.

"I never questioned what I needed to do. I left my life and..." he trailed off, gazing into the distance.

"... Honored your father's legacy." Aminah completed his unspoken sentence.

Nicolas nodded, shifting his gaze to her, staring a moment too long. He wanted to kiss her. Devour those luscious ass lips but Aminah had kept him in the friend zone for so long, he was uncertain of her desires.

"Come on. I have a surprise for you," Nicolas blurted, changing the subject.

"Surprise? Nic, I'm not the kinda girl who enjoys surprises." Aminah scrunched her button nose.

He stepped closer to her, leaving only space for a whisper of wind to separate them. Lowering his head to hers, Nic sprinkled a sweet peck on her nose.

"Lovie," he practically groaned.

"Let me see what I can do to change that," he exclaimed as a lustful smile curved the corners of his mouth.

"Can you come... please, Love?"

"Yes," she croaked, floating to him like a woman possessed.

3

Nic and Aminah aimlessly navigated the winery grounds. The moon cast an ember hue over the land as the sun faded to slumber. Lamp posts flickered to life, illuminating their path. Aminah was in awe of what appeared to be miles of grapevines weaved through the landscape.

Every structure held a rustic charm. So much history of heartache and triumph lived within the craftsmanship of the buildings and future harvests on these grounds. The sweet scent of fermented grapes perfumed the night air. Nic's firm grasp on her hand and gentle stroke of his thumb across her knuckles was filled with anticipation. Aminah was uncertain of Nic's surprise, but this... The secluded haven they shared was all of the surprise she needed.

"We're here?"

Aminah followed his eyes. Her wide grin warmed his heart.

"Oh my god, what is this?" she screeched, referring to the large oak tree beautifully brightened by countless fireflies.

What appeared to be thousands of them, swarmed in a choreographed dance shining a romantic hue of glitter and gold over the scenery.

"Why are there so many of them?" she asked, desperate to reach out and touch them.

Nic shrugged.

"I'm not sure. For as long as I can remember, every year around this time they put on a show," he chortled.

Aminah's copper eyes pranced to the synchronous sparkle created by the unique creatures.

"My dad used to say it's their mating ritual," Nic said.

Her eyes lifted in wonder.

"Evidently, each firefly flashes a unique pattern of light to attract their mate. The female waits patiently until she finds the perfect light show, while the male flies all over the place trying to impress the female," he chuckled, raising his brow.

"That sounds about right," Aminah giggled.

They lingered silently while Aminah admired the magical setting and Nic admired her.

"This place is enchanting," she voiced in a low-pitch, almost whisper-like.

"And you're beautiful," he hummed.

Stepping behind her, he instinctively glided his imposing hands around her waist, drawing her nearer. Nic nestled his nose in the curve of her neck. Aminah's eyes lazily lowered as her body relaxed into him. A gentle breeze rustled, carrying with it every unspoken *I love you* from him, and *I need you* from her.

Inhaling, he smelled the scent of fear and fervor simmering from her silky skin. Nic drizzled tiny kisses along her nape, paying special attention to the slope behind her ear.

He kissed then groaned, "Lovie."

Aminah freed a shaky breath but she did not move. She was paralyzed but felt the intensity of the caress and every ounce of his desire. Her pussy was drowning, suffocating under his embrace. The pound in the apex of her clit was frantic... agonizing.

Nic gently nibbled along the curve of her ear before gliding the tip of his tongue along the folds. Her legs trembled, battling between what she needed versus what she wanted. Aminah needed to get the hell out of there, but the countless glasses of wine mixed with her recent cravings for Nic rendered her weak.

Slowly spinning her around, Nic leaned in, resting his lips against hers. After all these years, this was their first kiss, which was *spectacular*. No tongues, no chaotic lust, just delicate and sweet. He sprinkled her lips with tiny kisses for what felt like an eternity. Gliding his hand to her hair, he fisted a handful of faux locs as he parted her mouth with his tongue.

"Nic," Aminah breathily whispered.

He wasn't sure if that was his queue to keep going or back away but his instinct told him that his Lovie was not ready. Pulling away, he rested his head on hers. Wordless, they stared at each other surrounded by the flashing fireflies.

"Are you game for one more surprise?" he breathed, disrupting their muted connection.

Aminah blinked, vainly attempting to conceal her shiny eyes that housed unshed tears.

She nodded.

Aminah was in her head and she was thankful that Nic could sense it. He grabbed her hand, kissing her fingertips, then muttered, "Follow me, Love."

Blushing, she followed his lead. Every time that word left his mouth something unexplainable happened to her.

Overflow, she mused, referring to her leaking, traitorous treasure. *But we're just friends. That's it, that's all.* Aminah continued to silently spew those lies.

Since Malakai, nobody penetrated her heart or pierced her mind. Not another human, *man or woman*. Yeah, woman.. that one brief moment of desperation and curiosity was an epic fail for Aminah.

But in the presence of Nicolas Touissant, the constant, debilitating grief she'd endured for the past several years evaporated. Daily visions of Malakai were exterminated at the sound of Nic's smooth baritone and the sight of his deep hickory eyes.

Over the years, reminiscing about her lost love had become another full time job. She could not escape his memory. He was everywhere: in her mind, her heart, her home, and the halls of the art school at Monroe University. So accepting a world that he didn't occupy felt like betrayal.

Kai was the love of your life. You promised him you would never love another. The saddened, grieving side of Aminah pondered.

Bitch, it's been too long. You betta let Nic's fine, thick ass knock the cobwebs off that pussy. The devilish, *Symphony-inspired* part of her surfaced.

Aminah snickered, shaking her head.

"Take off your shoes," Nic's gruff timbre shook her from the reverie.

"What?" she blurted, blinking rapidly.

"Take off your shoes." Nic requested again.

Aminah's curious eyes wandered throughout the space. Antique barrels and large machinery lined the walls of the oversized industrial room. A sizable wooden barrel filled with deep purple, almost black grapes was positioned in the center of the room.

"Nic, what are we doing here?"

"I gotta harvest a new fall wine and I need your help," he said, flashing her a gorgeous pearly-white dimpled smile.

"You wanna stomp some grapes with me, Love?" His hickory eyes pleaded, biting the corner of plump lips.

Shit! How could she resist that smile, those eyes, and his damn lips that she wanted to devour? Nicolas and Aminah had been playing with fire for far too long. Their relationship had far exceeded friends without the act of sex. The level of intimacy they shared often mirrored their married and dating friends.

Impassioned hugs, lustful gazes, and heightened care about each other's preferences. Nic knew not to get onions on Aminah's burgers, although she required a side of onion rings. While she corrected every waitress who added ice to his water. The adoration was mutual, yet complicated.

"Do people really still do this? I thought this was a myth. Some shit Sophia on *Golden Girls* talked about when she told her stories from Cicely," Aminah cackled.

Nic chuckled at her sentiment, uttering, "Nah, wineries don't really do this anymore. It's timely and not cost effective."

"And nasty. You forgot to mention that important fact," Aminah asserted, rolling her eyes in mock disgust.

"Actually, it's pretty sanitary once the grapes are processed," he said, placing a hand on the small of her back as they strolled through the room.

"Grape stomping is primarily for fun. Get a group of drunk chicks up in here stomping grapes on the weekends and I make a hell of a lot of money," Nic laughed, gleaning that Colgate smile.

"All of these expensive ass machines press the grapes to release the juice and begin the fermentation process. Saves me money, time, and purple feet." He joked as she admired the cutest damn smirk grace his face.

"Purple feet? Um, this is a fresh manicure, sir," Aminah teased.

"I got you. It'll be fun. Let's get you ready."

Nic nudged her to sit on the iron bench flanking the barrel. He dropped to a squat directly in front of Aminah. Her eyes traveled the length of his sturdy thighs to the imprint in his pants. She inhaled a deep breath. *Calm your little ass down, Minah.*

Cupping the back of her calf, he lifted her right leg centering it on his chest. Nic slowly, gently, unbuckled the strap of her silver Yves Saint Laurent sandals. He stroked a firm hand up her leg and placed her foot back on the floor.

Lifting her left leg, he repeated the tender perusal. Aminah's kitty was doused - dripping wet. She prayed he couldn't smell her personal aroma. Clearing her throat, she squirmed, vainly attempting to quell the tingle that scaled the walls of her essence.

Unlike Aminah, Nic withheld his response to how she made him feel. *Barely.* The knee length coral sundress offered just a glimpse of her curvy thighs but enough of a preview to have his dick throbbing. Nic reminisced on the times they'd fallen asleep together. How she'd swipe her bodacious thighs across his manhood in the middle of the night. *Shit!* He swallowed hard, endeavoring to minimize the tent forming in his shorts.

Nic placed the plastic covers on her feet then clasped her hands. Clutching her hands in his, he tugged gently, helping her stand up. He charmingly eyed her before planting a sweet kiss against her temple.

Aminah closed her eyes, inhaling him for just a second longer.

"Nic, are you sure about this?"

"Do you trust me?" he asked, lifting her chin to kiss against the scar that he never inquired about.

"I do," Aminah whimpered.

Chills invaded his flesh at the sound of '*I do*' escaping her lips.

But she wants to be just friends, he continually reminded himself. Nic thought it was bullshit, but it was her preference and he would follow her lead.

Nicolas stepped into the barrel first, but Aminah didn't follow. He extended his hands, pleading for her to join him.

She reluctantly obliged.

Aminah shivered from the cool, mushy sensation of the grapes. She stood motionless, uncertain of what to do next.

"Siri, queue music," Nic hailed.

Aminah smiled with recognition as she hummed to the sounds of Snoh Aalegra blaring from the surround sound speakers.

"Come here, Love."

Aminah carefully took a few steps towards him. She grasped his shirt, willingly folding into him.

"There's nothing to it. Just move," Nic instructed, hands clutched at the small of her back, encouraging the passionate sway.

They resided in that affectionate connection for what felt like a lifetime. The music was creating the soundtrack of their relationship as Yuna sang about having a crush. Although Aminah refused to admit it, she had more than a little crush on Nicolas Touissant.

"He Loves Me" by Jill Scott resounded. Aminah inhaled his sandalwood scent, weakened by the strength of his caress. Head resting against his chest, she sealed her eyes so tight, fisting the fabric of his t-shirt as they danced. Rapid inhales and exhales exchanged to the rhythmic beat.

Aminah was adrift, unconsciously mouthing the words - her true feelings for Nic.

. . .

You got me feeling like the breeze, easy and free and lovely and new. Oh when you touch me I just can't control it. When you touch me, I just can't hold it. The emotion inside of me, I can feel it.

Nic's disorientation didn't go unnoticed. Goosebumps invaded his flesh from the slightest touch. She trailed her fingertips up and down the cords of his muscular arms, momentarily pausing to trace the intricacies of the sphinx tattoo on his forearm. Nicolas wanted to kiss her so fucking bad. Inhale her mouth, seizing the red gloss from those damn pouty lips.

The rhythm and blues serenade continued in the background as Nic fingered her chin and lifted her from his chest. His hickory orbs, coupled with her pretty brown eyes, pleaded, begging for her approval.

"Nic," Aminah crooned, swiping her fingertip across his lip.

Nic gingerly delivered sweet pecks, before nibbling against her bottom lip. Anticipating rejection, he kissed her sensually, yet slow as his knuckles massaged up and down the slope of her back.

"Aah," Aminah softly sighed, tightening her grip around his neck.

Opening her lips with his thick, long tongue, he made love to her mouth. Sucking and circling her tongue at a lagging, measured rhythm. Aminah hated that she wanted to moan. Hated that her brain and body were in a heavyweight brawl.

Malakai was trying his damndest to infiltrate the moment like he did at the firefly tree but she was completely under Nic's spell. His kisses coupled with the gentle caress was a formula for a delicious disaster.

Loud. Aminah's whimpers grew louder when he licked then

kissed and licked then kissed down the arc of her neck, resting his lips at the swell of her breasts. She clutched his hands that firmly rested at the curves of her face. Dreamingly, yet unintentionally, she glided her leg up and down the length of his frame. Robust, stout, and so fucking hard, his dick gradually grew and grew, creeping up her stomach.

"Lovie. Shit," he murmured.

In one swift motion, Nic lifted her little bitty ass, encouraging those thickset thighs to wrap around his waist. Cupping her butt through the soft cotton fabric, he slouthily took careful steps backward to perch on the ledge of the barrel.

He intently, deeply, stared into her eyes. Sensually kissing while massaging through the soft fabric of her faux locs. The intensity of his kiss alone had her nearing a climax. But his hands kneading her ass discharged a guttural moan.

This was as far as they'd ever gone. As far as Aminah ever allowed. The few other times they danced on the edge of friendship and fucking was when she was high and had one too many drinks. Nic did not want her like that. He respected her too much. Hell, he *loved* her even more.

She tossed her head back between her shoulder blades, hands tightly clenched around his neck. Aminah grinded against the firmness of his manhood. His bulge pressed against the thin fabric of her lace thong. The unhurried pace of Aminah's movements contradicted the frenzy in her pussy.

"Nic. Nic. We should -. Oh my god."

It was too late to oppose. The pinnacle was upon her. The orgasm that bolted through her core was violently delicious. Two years lapsed since the last time a human brought her to orgasm. She tried to convince herself that the rose vibrator would sustain her needs, but that was bullshit. This man's dick was still in his pants, yet Aminah was spent as if he'd penetrated her ocean and fucked her into oblivion.

"I want you so damn bad, love. Just let go and let me take care of you."

Nic's ass was begging and he gave zero fucks about it. But he wasn't wrong. She wanted him... *bad.*

"What's keeping you away from me, Aminah?" His tone was a mix of a whisper and a groan.

She knew he was serious because he rarely called her Aminah. Her breathing was ragged. Fulfillment and peace were quickly vacating as anguish and anxiety moved in.

"Nic. I -" she halted, her words not aligning with her heart. Shit, or the orgasm she just experienced.

Aminah wasn't a crier so the overwhelming flood pooling in her eyes was jarring. She'd prevented herself from feeling anything for so long, the emotion was foreign.

"Nic. I can't."

The words were hushed but he heard them and obeyed. Just that fast, she flipped the switch and Nic was back in friend mode.

Aminah's swift recoil caused her to slip right out of his grasp. Her lace cladded ass fell right into the grapes. He assessed her mood before reacting. Was she hurt? Pissed? Embarrassed? Amused?

A lively giggle was music to his ears. He laughed too, lifting from the seat, not attempting to conceal his manly expanse. Even through all of her wavering and mysteriousness, Aminah was his friend. They'd had some good times together, and Nic did not want to lose her. Under any circumstance.

Bending to retrieve her, he easily scooped her into his arms, covering them with grape juice remnants. Her smile was infectious and so was his. They studied each other for a long minute.

Aminah blinked, breaking the intense ogling as she shook juice from her fingertips.

With her still lounging in his arms, Nic bent his head and slurped one of her fingers into his mouth. She gasped, then swallowed hard. He sensually slid each dainty finger over his tongue, never parting from their stare. *Shit!* Now, more than grape juice was saturating her.

"I bet I'm the first date to fall ass first in the grapes, huh?" she exclaimed, nervously chuckling.

Nic's brow bunched, causing Aminah to quickly regret the word vomit. He carefully stepped out of the barrel before planting Aminah on her feet. He paused, surveying her. *What is it with this woman?* He pondered. One moment she's hot and bothered... in a good way, and then the next she's ice cold.

Searching her eyes, he sought answers to the shift in her demeanor. Aminah just reached a climax in his lap. Her ass was cradled in the palms of his hands and now she was asking about other *dates... Other women.*

Exhaling through a snicker, Nic aimlessly shook his head, giving himself a moment to gather his thoughts

"No. I've never brought another woman here."

"Not even Fallon?" she blurted.

This time spewing *destructive* word vomit.

Fallon was Nic's ex-fiancée; a topic he rarely discussed and Aminah was well aware of that.

"Not even Fallon." His tone was a whisper, but he delivered his point matter-of-factly.

"But we don't date, remember? That's not what we do, right? We're just friends," Nic spat irritably.

Aminah slowly nodded, spiking her brows disbelievingly.

"Your rules, not mine, Aminah," Nic said and the vexation in his tone was tight.

Aminah. He never calls me Aminah. I may as well be Ms. Loveless, she thought. Anything other than *love* or *lovie* coming from his luscious lips insulted her.

Nic motioned his head for her to follow him to the water sprayer. Muted, he cleaned her legs and feet. Those beautiful hickory eyes turned several shades darker when he was pissed off. They were almost the color of coal at this point.

"Let's go back to the house so you can get cleaned up," he scoffed, refusing to make eye contact.

"Nic," Aminah tried.

"It's getting late. We should go," he said dryly, marching towards the exit.

The walk back to his house was tense. As usual, Nic was a gentleman, clasping her hand to ensure she safely navigated the trails through the vineyard. But he was silent. Simply put, Nic was angry and maybe even a little hurt.

While he and Aminah had not defined their connection, they were, at minimum, friends. Friends with an undeniable attraction to each other.

Climbing the steps, Nic showed Aminah to his sister's room. She stood in the middle of the space, circling her eyes around the chic-styled bedroom sprinkled with childhood memorabilia.

"Here you go," Nic said, extending his hand to offer Aminah a t-shirt and shorts.

"There's soap and fresh towels in Nomi's bathroom." He continued, pointing to the ensuite restroom.

Aminah nodded.

"I'll be quick so I can get out of your hair."

That was not what she wanted to say but they were the only words that could be verbalized in the moment.

"It's almost midnight, Aminah. I'm not allowing you to drive back to Monroe tonight. This room is yours for the night. Make yourself comfortable."

"Not allowing me?" Aminah's neck rolled back.

"That's what I said. It's not up for discussion. Goodnight, Love."

Nic kissed her cheek then left the room. Aminah stood stunned. Ogling the empty doorway, she wanted to run after him and offer a few more black girl neck rolls while giving him the litany of reasons why he can't speak to her that way. But she knew he was right... *about everything.*

After her shower, she tried to sleep but her mind was spinning. She needed some fresh air. Gingerly, Aminah crept through the more than one hundred year old house, trying to navigate under the dimmed lights by memory. Tiptoeing down the stairs, she heard the faint sound of piano keys floating down the hallway. Every room on the first floor was dark except for one.

Barefoot, Aminah crept towards the melodic sound. Nicolas was seated at a mahogany piano that appeared just as vintage as the house. It was beautiful. *He* was beautiful. Nic was bare from the waist, with only black lounge pants covering his athletic frame. He wasn't overly cut but his time in the military had done a body good. The intricate art of the arm tattoo trailed a path down his back. With every stroke of the keys his muscles tensed. *Damn.*

Sensing a presence in the room, Nic uttered, "Did I wake you?"

Aminah shook her head as if he could see her.

He spun around on the piano bench and was momentarily breathless. Even in a basic tee and shorts, Aminah was breathtaking. She carried this hardcore, unflinching persona for the most part, but she was bashful and broken in quiet moments like now. Beautifully so, but broken, nonetheless.

"No. I couldn't sleep. And I think your dog is missing his auntie."

At the mention of a dog, a beautiful chocolate labrador retriever appeared in the doorway.

"Come on, Cab," Nic said, patting his leg twice.

Slowly, the dog trotted towards Nic and rested beside the piano.

"Cab," Aminah snickered, questioningly.

Nic nodded.

"Short for Cabernet," he said, shrugging. "Like the wine."

Aminah giggled, "Aww, that's cute."

"My dad's idea. Me and Nomi wanted to name her Espresso."

"She's sweet. She just laid in the doorway, looking at me."

"Yeah, she knows not to go into Naomi's room without permission. It's always been that way," Nic said, bending to stroke his hand down the dog's deep brown fur.

"How old is she?" Aminah asked, still loitering at the entry of the room.

"Old," he chuckled.

Nic watched as Aminah's eyes slowly perused his favorite room in the house. Antique furniture filled the space with gold, heavy curtains hanging at the oversized windows. The corner fireplace held so much charm, appearing original to the house. A large wooden china cabinet with intricate carvings in the glass doors stood at least eight feet tall. The fixture was filled with antique place settings and wine glasses. Next to it was a matching cabinet filled with bottles of Touissant wine. Some bottles appeared to be older than her.

"Do you require permission to enter the room as well?" Nic asked, teasingly.

He patted the space next to him on the bench, motioning for her to come closer. Aminah strode across the room as she admired the space's history. Sliding next to him, she flashed a toothless smile.

Her coyness was sexy to a man like Nic. In his world, the coquettishness was like foreplay. During those rare occasions of vulnerability, Aminah demonstrated her most honest, forthcoming and affectionate persona with him.

"Play me something," Aminah instructed with a sugary tone.

"Any requests?" he inquired.

She shook her head.

Nic swayed his body from side to side to get comfortable. With his head lifted and eyes lowered, he tickled the keys until he settled on a melody. Once she recognized the tune, Aminah instinctively swayed, too. With closed eyes, she hummed the chorus.

What felt like a lifetime ticked by as Nic effortlessly navigated the complicated chords. To her surprise, Nic complemented her humming by crooning about never feeling a way about loving. He was no Brian McKnight, but Nic could sing.

Unable to look at her, Nic sang from his gut, allowing the lyrics to narrate his affections.

There will never come a day, you'll ever hear me say, that I want and need to be without you.

I wanna give my all. Baby just hold me. Simply control me.

Cause your arms, they keep away the loneliest.

When I look into your eyes, then I realize that all I need is you in my life.

All I need is you in my life, cause I... Never felt this way about loving.

Aminah could not take her eyes off of him. Everytime she tried to avert her stare, it was as if an invisible force compelled her to return her eyes to him. She gazed watchfully, unable to break the spell he casted. Fixation, yearning... *Love* lived in the creases of his handsome face.

But she recognized something else... pain. Aminah's breath hitched, eyes brimming with unspoken sorrow, threatening to spill over at any moment. She'd done this. She was the root of his angst.

Nic played the final notes of the song softly before he unhurriedly opened his eyes. His gaze softened when he noticed a tear slip still down her reddened cheek.

"Why are you crying, Love?"

Aminah shook her head. She swiped away the traitorous tears aggressively, betraying her attempt to remain composed.

"I'm sorry," she apologized.

"For..." he said, lifting her chin to see those pretty copper eyes.

She faltered as a distressing pout curled the corners of her mouth. Aminah's eyes revealed all of her secrets. They were the windows to her soul and Nic saw the silent language that spoke volumes.

"That I'm so fucked up," she snickered warily.

"That I can't be what you want," Aminah croaked, licking the salted tears from her mouth.

Although years had passed, heart wrenching images of Malakai immediately darkened her soul like one of his painfully beautiful canvases. Aminah's grief and guilt was like a tangled web, entwined in a suffocating embrace. Nicolas was aware of her past love, but he had no clue about the extent of the heart wrenching end of Aminah and Malakai.

"Lovie… do you even know what I want?" he interrogated but didn't wait for a response.

Nic shifted to straddle the bench and scooted closer to her. So connected, their hearts beat in sync with each other's rhythm.

Gently nudging her thighs, he hoisted Aminah to straddle him. She didn't object. Her elbows clashed with the piano keys, causing the most captivating and chaotic sound, a sample of their love song. Their relationship was a bittersweet symphony, each note tinted with the ache of adoration and the euphoria of profound passion.

"I want *you,* Aminah Rae Loveless. I want *us*… forever."

4

Aminah sipped on another glass of red wine from Touissant Winery as she admired her friend, Symphony, and new husband, Tyus, swaying on the dance floor. Surprised was an understatement when she received a video call from her best friends asking her to help them plan a surprise wedding.

She'd just entered her place after an emotional night with Nic in Brighton Falls.

I want us forever. Aminah pondered his words. *Nic, I'm sorry. I can't.* She despised hers.

Nic and forever was the perfect harmony for a girl not tethered to her past. But Aminah carried a constant reminder of the sacrifices she swore to uphold. In Nic's presence, the promise she made was a relic of a past she didn't recognize, but she was still torn between honoring her word and following the desires of her heart.

"Let's welcome The Okoros back to the dance floor," the DJ's voice boomed through the microphone, jerking Aminah from her haze.

The gleam on Tyus's face narrated every sentiment he carried for his new wife. He wanted to make Symphony his as soon as they declared their love for each other. But Symphony was being her stubborn self until she was faced with losing her once in a lifetime love.

In true Symphony fashion, she made a bold move and planned a surprise wedding. When Tyus returned home from a golf outing on his birthday, he was greeted by roughly fifty of their closest family and friends positioned in their backyard to witness them declare their love to each other. It was one of the most romantic gestures and intimate wedding ceremonies Aminah had ever seen.

Symphony looked like she was literally about to pop but glowed with joy at thirty-plus weeks pregnant. Aminah smiled, blinking back tears, as her other best friend, Syncere, glided across her view wrapped in the arms of her husband, King.

Years ago, Aminah didn't believe she would witness fairytale love stories for her best friends. Her stubborn friends fought their chances at love kicking and screaming until they met their Prince Charmings.

Aminah's slight beam blossomed to a wide smile while reminiscing about the first day they'd met during freshman orientation at Monroe University over fifteen years ago. Since then, she'd been through hell and back with these girls. They were her rocks. Her earth and fire, because she was their wind.

Her friends had found unconditional love and for a mere second, she blinked back tears, wishing she was floating in their shoes. That thought quickly diminished because she had experienced this kind of love, but it was gone. *He* was absent but never forgotten.

"May I have this dance, Love?"

Aminah quickly spun around, causing the wine glass to tip over on the table. The familiar throaty, bass-filled tenor jolted her from the reminiscence. She calmed as the corners of her mouth curved slightly and a blush reddened her cheeks. Just that fast, the recollection of her *once-upon-a-time* love was momentarily paused at the sound of what was possible.

Nicolas.

He stood before her draped in terra cotta-colored skin that literally looked like it was permanently kissed by the sun. Thick, dark brown tapered waves made her seasick, and the deep dimple peeking through the matching beard made her ready to jump overboard. Aminah hadn't seen him in a few weeks, and she missed the caress of his stocky athletic structure.

He was her possibility. A second chance kinda love. But during the winery getaway, Nic made it crystal clear that he wanted answers. He wasn't asking for much, other than a commitment to the possibility of a future between them. But Aminah could not offer that. Not with Malakai haunting her.

"Aminah, if I had it my way, you would be mine. My woman and one day, my wife. I understand that's not where you are, but you feel something for me, otherwise, you wouldn't be here. Not like this," Nic expressed.

With Aminah straddled across his lap on the piano bench, he stared deep into her glazed eyes.

"Do you feel anything for me? Is there space for me in here, Love?" he questioned, tapping her chest, signifying her heart.

Aminah nodded her head. Her body quaked from the storm of cries raging. They threatened to consume her from the inside out, but she could not reveal the truth of her disquietude.

"It's like there's something you want to say to me but you're holding back. You've trusted me with your fears, secrets, and hopes for the

future... Why can't you let me in here?" he uttered, pointing to her head before swiping away a stray tendril.

"Trust me with your heart, Aminah."

Aminah squirmed a bit to quiet the memory and the growing throb in her middle before turning to acknowledge him. She lifted the wine glass to her lips, wishing for another sip because she needed a little liquid courage before shifting to gaze into big eyes the color of baked clay.

"Hi," she uttered sweetly.

"Hi, Lovie. How have you been?" Nic's baritone was powerful but soft at the same time.

"Pretty good. How are you?"

Nic shrugged, then took a swig of his drink. Placing the glass on the table, he leaned against it then crossed his arms over his chest.

"I've been better."

Aminah nodded but could not say a word. She knew that she was the cause and likely the cure for his woes.

"I'm sor -" He halted her apology, placing two fingers over her lips.

Her big eyes stared up at him. Nic shook his head.

"No apologies needed, Love."

Nic clasped her hands in his then lifted them to his lips. One peck, then two.

"Instead of an apology, you know how you can make it better?"

She shook her head.

"Dance with me," he said, extending his elbow for her to grab.

"It would be my pleasure, Mr. Touissant," she replied, giggling.

Nic kissed the top of her hand again and gently flipped it over to plant his lips onto her palm. He just always made things better. He connected their fingers and pulled her into a smooth sway on the makeshift dance floor in Tyus and Symphony's backyard.

Nic gazed at Aminah as she swayed towards the middle of the dance floor with their fingers interlocked. He was jealous of how the white dress hugged her curves. Spinning her around, he dropped a soft peck to her exposed shoulder while pulling her closer.

As Kem sang "I Can't Stop Loving You," Nic bit his bottom lip to prevent echoing the song's words. He had never in his life battled this hard for a woman. But the first time his eyes landed on Aminah, all of his certainty about not wanting marriage and babies quickly faded. Nic saw *forever* in her eyes. He flashed a sexy closed-mouth smile.

"You're staring," she softly murmured, blushing.

"You're beautiful," he retorted.

She blushed.

"Join me for a nightcap," Nic asked.

Aminah beamed because a nightcap with him always included dessert, a bottle of delicious wine from his family's winery, and a gentle scalp massage as she slept on his chest, absent of any nightmares.

"Right now?" she inquired.

He nodded.

"The party is winding down. Symphony looks like she's about to go into labor and Syncere and King act like they're about to consummate their marriage all over again. So, yeah... now."

Aminah chuckled.

"Can this nightcap include butter pecan ice cream?" she teased.

"Two scoops *with* caramel drizzle... Absolutely." He winked.

"Oh, yes. Don't threaten me with a good time, sir," she laughed. "Let me grab my stuff."

Striding across the emptying backyard into the house, matching gray eyes paused Aminah's rapid pursuit. Syncere snatched her by the hand while Symphony waddled behind them down the hallway. They closed the bedroom door and immediately interrogated her.

"Did you tell him?" Syncere inquired, with her hands propped on her hips.

"Now you know she didn't," Symphony chimed, carefully sitting in the oversized chair.

She kicked up one foot then motioned for Syncere to remove her shoes as she continued.

"If Nic knew that she was leaving for four months, he would not be looking like the sun, moon, and stars resides in this girl's ass," Symphony bantered.

Aminah rolled her eyes.

"No. I haven't told him yet. I will tonight. Besides, Nic is not my man. I can come and go as I please and I've made the decision to go," Aminah whined.

"Ok, well, if you're so big and bad, why won't you tell him?" Syncere challenged, leering at her friend.

Aminah was hushed.

"You and Nic have been joined by the hip for years. You know what he wants from you Minah," Syncere fussed.

"What Syncere?" Aminah questioned but Nic had already disclosed the answer.

"You, bitch," Symphony shouted, rolling her eyes.

Syncere shook her head. Symphony wasn't wrong, but her approach always leaned heavier on the aggressive side.

"Stop doing this to yourself, friend. Nic loves you. Yes, as his friend, but he wants so much more. And I believe that you want the same too," Syncere said in a much gentler tone.

Aminah sighed, swiping away a stray tear. She shook her head.

"You both know I cannot do that. I can't give him that. Not right now at least."

Silence fell over the trio momentarily as they pondered their common threads. *Secrets and trauma.*

Syncere tackled the PTSD triggered by her rape daily, while Symphony still struggled with her abandonment issues, but they were both managing through therapy and the love of two great men.

Aminah, on the other hand, used *avoidance* as her therapy of choice. She preferred to pretend - live a falsified reality.

"Minah, we know what you are dealing with and we don't mean to minimize it, but, sweetie, you have to make some decisions for yourself. *You* deserve to find love again, boo," Syncere said, sitting next to her friend on the edge of the bed.

"Listen, I'm only fussing at you because you deserve the world, Mi. Whether it's Nic or somebody else, I just want you to be happy," Symphony cried.

"I almost lost Tyus because I was being stupid. Pretending like I did not need him. But God knows I would be crazy without that man. Don't wait until it's too late," Symphony advised.

Silence lingered again for what felt like an eternity. Aminah wiped her face one last time, then hopped off the bed.

"I'll tell him tonight," she announced.

Her friends knew she was likely lying but did not say a word. Symphony shook her head, while Syncere simply watched as Aminah gathered her things.

"My wedding was beautiful though, right?" Symphony blurted.

"Right," Aminah and Syncere squealed in unison.

The hush was quickly replaced with giddy banter as they swooned over the wedding ceremony and reception. A light tap at the door quieted their giggles.

"I am looking for my wife," Tyus roared playfully.

"Here I am, husband," Symphony sang.

Tyus eyed her and even with a bulging belly, puffy nose, and swollen feet, the love and lust for his wife was oozing from him. He stealthily crossed the room looking fine as hell in a fitted tan suit. Symphony nibbled the corner of her bottom lip as she gawked his amble towards her.

Tyus bent to speak directly in her face.

"Mrs. Okoro, are you ready to consummate this marriage?" he posed, then kissed her temple.

"Yeess, Daddy," Symphony squealed. "As soon as you help me up," she chuckled.

Tyus carefully lifted his very pregnant wife to a standing position. Once Symphony was on her feet, he kissed her forehead, nose then lips and whispered, "I love you, Symphony Okoro."

"I love you, Tyus Okoro, Sr."

Tyus and Symphony headed towards the door to exit when he paused.

"Syn, your husband and children are looking for you," he said, eyeing Syncere, then darted his gaze to Aminah.

"Minah, Nic is waiting for you. He's in the living room."

She nodded.

"Don't go into labor tonight being nasty, prima," Syncere chuckled.

"I can't make any promises," Symphony yelped as she headed down the hall.

They all boisterously laughed.

Aminah shook her head as she resumed gathering her belongings. Syncere walked towards the bedroom door when she heard the soft whimpers of her baby boy whining to his daddy about not being ready to go to sleep.

Momentarily hesitating, she quietly muttered, “Minah,” gaining her friend’s attention.

Aminah paused, lifting her eyes to her friend.

“I’ll pick you up in the morning,” Syncere said.

Aminah nodded.

“Tell him, Mi.” Syncere requested again but she knew her effort was in vain.

Aminah swiftly bobbed her head.

Watching the door to ensure Syncere was gone, she stopped packing for a second and dropped her face into the palms of her hand. One deep breath in, followed by an audible gasp repeated for about sixty seconds.

She grabbed her phone and navigated to the contact she’d avoided all day. Aside from Nic, this call was the last loop to close before she left for London.

“Mrs. Bradley,” Aminah said questioningly once she heard the voice on the other end of the phone.

“Aminah.” A woman’s raspy voice spoke in the same questioning tone.

“Yes, ma’am. How are things?”

“Mmm... As well as expected,” the woman replied with the same response she gave every time Aminah called.

“What can I do for you? It’s been awhile.”

Aminah nodded.

“Yeah. Work is keeping me busy. I was calling to let you know that I’ll be out of the country for a few months. London,” she said, clearing the lump forming in her throat.

"Everything is taken care of but if there's an emergency, you can call me."

"Ok. I'm sure everything will be fine. Safe travels, Aminah. I hope this is for fun. Some time for you," the woman said.

"Yeah. Thank you, Mrs. Bradley."

After hanging up, Aminah resumed her deep breathing, whispering to herself.

"Get it together, Aminah. Get it together."

Slipping into the flats, she grabbed her bags and exited the bedroom. Slowly trekking down the hall, she gave herself a few more minutes to ensure her facade was in place.

The Okoro and Cartwright families were gathered at the front door near the living room. Delight and laughter filled their faces. Jealousy and joy battled as Aminah stared at the happy couples. Nic quickly shifted his stance as if he could sense her ogling. He smiled, but it soon morphed into a questioning smirk in response to her demeanor.

Nic excused himself from the group then began walking towards her. He reached to retrieve her bag.

"You good?" he asked.

She nodded.

"Words, Lovie," Nic requested.

"Yes, I'm good. I'm ready whenever you are."

"Are you sure?" he asked, stroking his thumb across her forearm.

She nodded again with a smile.

"I'm sure."

Nic nipped the tip of her nose then smiled. They said their final goodbyes then strolled to his car. Nicolas opened the passenger door to help her into the car before placing her bag in the trunk. She settled into the plush leather seats, expecting at least a thirty minute drive to the downtown hotel where Nic usually stayed when he was in Haven. But the journey was less than fifteen minutes since they hadn't left the city.

Turning into a driveway off Main Street, Nic parked his truck and motioned for Aminah to get out. Her face was laced with confusion.

"Nic, where are we?"

"It's a surprise. Come on," he chuckled, extending his hand to her.

Aminah lifted a questioning brow but clutched his hand anyway. Nic walked slightly ahead of her, retrieving keys from his pocket. He glanced back at Aminah and laughed because endless questions lived in the crinkles on her forehead.

"Trust me, Lovie."

Nic unlocked the back door and pressed a few buttons to brighten the space. Large boxes marked heavy and shrink-wrapped equipment crowded the room. Aminah's eyes danced around the room but he'd swept her into another area before she could fix her mouth to probe.

More lights illuminated and Aminah's breath hitched when she noticed the Touissant logo painted on the concrete wall.

"Nic," she squeaked questioningly.

"Welcome to the very first *Grapes and Mash*," he exclaimed, smiling from ear to ear.

"Nic. Oh my god. This is amazing."

Aminah practically jumped into his arms.

"You did it. I'm so proud of you."

Nic spun her around, burying his nose in the crook of her neck. Aminah giggled, allowing her head to fall back in delight, recalling when this concept was just a random thought in his head.

During a weekend visit to Monroe, Aminah took Nic to The Caverns for a picnic. They often chatted about their wildest dreams, and that night, he mentioned that wine wasn't his passion; it was just a family tradition.

"I want to start something new. Something that holds my name beyond just my father and grandfather's legacies," he said, as they watched a group of kids playing.

"Something new like what," Aminah probed, popping a cube of cheese into her mouth.

He gazed at her, loving how she was genuinely interested in the desires of his heart.

"I've been dabbling in distilling whiskey at the winery. We've served it during dinner on the weekends and it's getting solid reviews."

"Nicolas, are we keeping secrets?"

Aminah dramatically rested a hand against her chest, feigning outrage.

He chuckled. "Nah, never that, Love. I just... I don't know."

"You do know. Tell me," she encouraged, nudging his shoulder.

"I want to open a wine and whiskey spot. A bar that serves only specialty Toussant wine and my whiskey. I want it to have an old school tavern vibe."

Aminah nodded, focused on his every word.

"What would you call it?" she asked.

Nic narrowed his eyes, hesitant to share what he'd been plotting.

"Ok, promise me you won't laugh," he said, tossing up his pinky finger.

Aminah looked at his finger then lifted her gaze to him. The seriousness in his stare was so damn sexy.

Joining her pinky finger with his, she vowed, "I promise."

Nic pulled their adjoined fingers to his lips and delicately kissed at the joint. Aminah's breath hitched. It was a simple exchange but dripped with intimacy.

"Grapes and Mash," he uttered, never disjoining his eyes from hers.

Aminah swallowed hard, blinking rapidly to return to the moment.

"Huh?"

"I would name it Grapes and Mash," Nic repeated.

"I like the sound of it but what does that mean?"

"I think my reason for using grapes is pretty self-explanatory," he snickered teasingly.

Aminah rolled her eyes and nodded.

"Mash is a combination of ingredients used to make alcohol. Whiskey is made from fermented mash. So... Grapes and Mash. It will still have the Touissant brand, but the concept is mine."

"That's amazing, Nic. What's stopping you?"

"I don't want to fail," he said matter-of-factly.

"I recall a really good friend of mine telling me that failing makes the success that much greater. Now who was that? Hmm... I believe his name is Nicolas Touissant," she buzzed playfully.

"Touche. Touche," he said, lifting his hands in surrender.

"I manifest that it will happen for you. You'll never know unless you try, Nic," she uttered, nudging her shoulder against his.

"Thank you. And thank you for the encouragement. I appreciate it more than you know," he said, resting his lips on her forehead.

"Anytime. When do you open?"

"If everything goes as planned with the permits... a couple months," he responded, beaming.

Aminah's smile matched his then slightly faltered when he asked, "You'll be there, right? Opening night." He clarified.

She took a deep breath and quickly nodded. Aminah kept a secret that would likely prevent her from being there but Nic's excitement was contagious. He pinched the tip of her nose, causing her to wrinkle her face, feigning annoyance, but she loved all of his expressions of affection.

"You ready for that nightcap?" he asked.

She nodded and he laughed, guiding her towards the back door. After locking the door, he walked Aminah to the passenger side of his truck and they headed down Main Street for ice cream.

"Where are you staying?" he asked, while they waited for their order.

"Syncere's."

"Do you want to eat here, then I can take you back?" he probed while retrieving the order from the server.

He nodded a muted thanks and grabbed the paper bag.

She shook her head.

Nic paused, not prepared for her wordless response.

"What do you want to do, Love?"

Aminah's eyes held words that her lips were terrified to speak. As usual for the pair, longing, desire and uncertainty danced between their silent exchanges.

Stumbling over her words, she muttered, "I... um... I want to stay with you, Nic."

The fidgeting of fingers and rapid blinking of her eyes signaled unease. Her round, sparkling orbs were a tumultuous whirlwind, swirling with equal parts love and fear. Nic had witnessed this before in his lovie, but something else was brewing in the cloudy sea of her eyes. *Want. Consent.*

Nic eyed her lustfully yet warily. She had never made this request before, and he was usually the primary initiator of their encounters. For Aminah to vocally express her need for his company was… new… refreshing.

"Of course, Love. You never have to ask."

5

Minutes later, Nic pulled into the lot behind the building they had just left. Aminah's face was dressed with confusion and sleepiness. He exited the truck and opened her door.

"You ready?"

"Why are we back here?" she probed, eyeing him suspiciously.

"You said you wanted to stay with me. This is my spot."

"Your spot?" she said curiously. "You're sleeping at your bar?"

Nic's laughter echoed through the night's air.

"No, Love. I'm sleeping in the studio apartment of *my* building."

"*Your* building," she screeched, excitedly hopping out of the truck.

He nodded.

Nic usually got a hotel suite when he visited his friends in Haven Pointe. With his new business adventure, he would be spending long days and nights at the bar, so it only made sense to have a permanent place.

"When I toured the space, the realtor mentioned that the owner wanted to relinquish it all for the right price. The bar space is actually two small storefronts that I combined and there's two apartments upstairs. They need some work but a good investment."

Aminah stared at him. She was completely in awe of this man. Speechless, she followed his lead through the back entrance and up one flight of stairs. The short hallway was flanked with two doors. He walked to the door with the gold number one plastered on to the peeling paint.

Entering, her brows peeked, thinking that this place was a far cry from his home in Brighton Falls. The first features that caught her attention were tall, vaulted ceilings and massive square footage. The apartment was studio-style, with no walls separating the spaces other than the bathroom and closet.

A king-sized bed and nightstand were pushed against the furthest wall in front of the large bay window. Boxes were scattered throughout and papers cluttered a table near the kitchen that seemingly doubled as a desk. The kitchen was fully equipped but other than those items, the space was bare.

"I wasn't expecting company," Nic shrugged, heeding the scrutinizing expression on her face.

"It's nice," Aminah giggled with a disbelieving smirk.

He eyeballed her and seconds later they harmoniously released a boisterous laugh.

"Ok, ok. It needs a little work but it has potential," she said, following him into the kitchen.

"Is the other apartment occupied?"

Nic shook his head.

"No. I have a contractor working on it so I can rent it within the next few months."

"This place is massive. Is the other unit this big?" she continued to probe.

"Are you trying to be my neighbor, Lovie?" Nic winked.

Aminah darted squinted eyes away from the final perusal of his new home to look at him.

"Maybe," she teased.

"Don't play with me, Love. I will start painting shit right now," he laughed.

"I'm definitely considering a change but not sure what just yet," she said.

"Could Haven be a part of that change?"

Aminah shrugged.

"Haven could be in my future plans. We'll see," she uttered.

Her voice was small but he heard every word. Nic's brow peeked, excitement dancing across his handsome face.

"I said maybe," she giggled, playfully pushing his arm.

"Well, I have a place for you whenever you're ready to make that move." Nic nudged her chin.

Aminah blushed, kicking her bare feet while perched on the kitchen island. Nic settled beside her as they chatted about nothing important and laughed about everything as they enjoyed their ice cream. Her spoon dipped into his butter pecan a few times, but he received the death glare anytime he attempted to taste her strawberry shortcake.

Nic yawned while his muscular arms stretched, still draped in his wedding attire. He'd removed his jacket and shoes but was more than ready to rid himself of the fitted shirt and slacks. Blinking rapidly, he rubbed a hand down his face before unbuttoning his shirt.

"I'm losing steam, Love," he growled through another yawn.

Aminah nodded, discharging a yawn of her own.

"Me too," she declared, stretching her arm before signaling him to help her down from the countertop.

Nic shook his head with a faint, but sexy smirk on his face.

"Big baby," he joked.

"Mm-hmm," she hummed.

Nic's hands slowly slipped across the silky fabric of the bridesmaid dress when he snaked his arms around her waist. He desperately wanted to cup her ass but he remained a gentleman. Gently lifting her from the marble, Nic drank in her intoxicating scent. The sweet, floral aroma tickled his senses like a fine wine.

Aminah allowed the tip of her nose to graze up and down his cheek. He smelled so damn good all of the time, but tonight, every inhale of the crisp, woodsy scent dispatched shivers through her center. She was mesmerized, falling deeper into his spell.

Nic often joked that Aminah was practicing witchery the way she had him chasing it with no future relationship. But Aminah knew that Nicolas was *in fact* a sorcerer sprinkling manly magic all over their relationship... friendship... Their *complication.*

"So I guess you want me to carry you," he said, recognizing that she'd draped her thick, curvy legs around his body.

"Mm-hmm," she hummed again.

Aminah did not want to speak too many words because she feared it would deter her from tonight's plan.... Make love to Nicolas Touissant. She was determined not to allow the silent whispers of objections to crowd her head. Aminah rejected the sensitivities of her heart because *love* for Nic was too much to fathom.

Tonight, she focused on listening to her body and it was screaming... *Nic, I want you to fuck me.* Or maybe Symphony's earlier message was beginning to resonate. "*Bitch, you betta see what that dick do before he gives your shit away.*"

Yep. Everyone, including Aminah, claimed Nic as hers. She knew it was absurd but she didn't care. Over the past several years, he'd been warm respite, an armor of protection and a perfectly sculpted shoulder to cry on.

Her family and friends always wanted to fix her woes, but Nic... simply listened with an open heart whenever she needed to pour out her troubles. He never provided solutions, only solace. Nicolas was a constant for her and consistently offered a heavy helping of compassion—and maybe even a little love.

Nic cradled Aminah, carrying her like a baby. She melted into him, finding comfort and familiarity in his touch. Their bodies were so enmeshed, they created the perfect mold. Nic chuckled softly at her protest when he tried to put her down.

"Lovie. You gotta get down."

"Ugh," she groaned, reluctantly settling on her feet.

Big, bold eyes stared at him, mutely orating her need.

"Can I help you?" he asked, trailing one finger down the zipper on the side of her dress.

She nodded.

Nic made quick work of the zipper before slipping the straps from her shoulder one at a time. Gradually, the fabric fell from her frame, requiring some prodding to slip over her ample hips. He was so damn gentle and delicate with her when she didn't always deserve it.

A one-piece shaper darker than her skin cloaked her beautiful body. Aminah was breathtaking. While sometimes quiet and coy, she exuded brazen confidence in her body. And damn, milk had done her body good.

Aminah's figure curved in all of the necessary places. Balancing softness and strength that left him breathless. Those damn brown eyes were pleading, begging for him to make the first move, but Nic was cautious. Shit, afraid.

He and his lovie had often overstepped actual and imaginary bounds since they'd met. So yeah, he was a bit trigger shy with her. Aminah was often like that puzzle box with a missing piece you would never solve but couldn't force yourself to discard.

"Let me find you something to sleep in," Nic blurted quickly because he needed to get the hell away from her for a second.

He loved everything about this woman. The way her hair fell across her shoulders when she removed the pins from the updo to the innocence misting her eyes. Aminah was frozen, just staring at him. Nic took one step to get around her when she grabbed his forearm.

"Nic," she croaked.

He surveyed her from the silky tresses to the arc of her plump ass. Nic had never wanted to metamorphose into a thong shaper as much as he did in that moment. Her ass was on full display for his viewing pleasure, and Aminah did not flinch.

The harmonious gaze they shared was unbreakable. Nic was completely entranced with this woman daily, but tonight, he was fucking fascinated. He'd promised not to let Aminah put him in this position again. *She's not ready.* But the way his dick pounded against his zipper, begging to be set free, he was about to renege on that vow.

Kissing her temple, his lips coasted down her face before he whispered in her ear.

"Just say the word, Love."

Aminah lifted lazy, lust-filled eyes to him.

With a soft sigh, she pressed her lips to his ear and uttered, "Word."

Nicolas cupped her chin firmly, forcing her head back to ensure her eyes were planted on him.

"Don't bullshit me. Are you sure? Because there's no going back, Aminah. If you get in this bed–" he paused, inhaling deeply with anticipation lacing his stare.

"If I am blessed enough to have you in my bed, Love, I'm taking my time. I want to taste and lick you everywhere. Once I'm inside you there's no going back, Ms. Loveless," he vehemently promised.

Her breath hitched as she wantonly screeched, "Nicolas."

Aminah knew what she was about to do but sadly didn't care. While she was certain about her decision, the weight of it still loomed over her. She would have to leave him behind to find herself but tonight, she yearned for just one more moment in his arms before saying goodbye.

Pressing his big body against hers, his momentum forced her backwards. The back of her legs pressed against the mattress and her knees buckled. Nic palmed her ass, catching her fall.

"I want you naked," he ordered.

One delicate kiss to her lips. And then another... And another. He gazed into her gorgeous copper eyes. Nic was bracing for her usual opposition. *Nic, wait. Nic, no we can't.* But nothing filled the room other than her raspy whimpers of expectancy.

Nic peeled the satin shaper from her flesh, section by section. He wanted to revel in this unveiling. Firm, round breasts with chocolate chips for nipples had him ready for a snack. Aminah stood willing and ready as she nibbled the corner of her bottom lip while she surveyed him, surveying her.

He caressed her breast so delicately as if he was handling the sweetest crop of grapes. With each stroke of his hand, every whisper of *Love,* Nic's foreplay was slow and tantalizing. He was taking Aminah on a journey and the first stop was intoxication. She was fucking drunk from the mere touch of this man's hands.

Nic had dreamed about this for years and he'd be damned if he was going to rush it. Ridding her of the last stitch of material, he regarded her body. Cataloging every inch of her frame from the arc of her neck, the dip of her waist, and the sway of her hips. She was a masterpiece and he was smitten - fucking drunk in love.

Aminah was unsure of what to do or say, so she did nothing but allow him to savor the sight. Nic began to undress, but he never retreated his stare. Their eyes flickered, igniting a spark that triggered a silent challenge. Their story was a duel between love and war. Nic was in love, while Aminah toiled with demons from her past.

Her eyes never faltered until... *Damn.*

Nic's pants and boxers hit the floor, exposing the muscle she'd been waiting to see. It was wide and rigid and wonderful. Just enough length to have her moaning until the wee hours of the night. She licked her lips, unable to contain the yearning to taste him.

The corner of his mouth curved into a sexy grin as if he knew what she was thinking. He shook his head while shortening the small gap between them.

"Nah, Love. I get the first taste."

Nic narrowed the space between them, stepping directly into the miniscule illumination from the light post outside the window.

She sucked in a breath while her eyes digested the intricacy of his arm tattoos. She'd seen them before but was never privy to the one in the center of his chest.

A red heart with a key opening in the center and the word *love* etched in a fancy script. With just one step forward, there was no longer a gap between them. No room for insecurities or uncertainties. She lifted dainty fingertips to his chest fingering the tattoo.

"Is this for me?"

Nic eyed her, a light snicker fell from his lips

"I only have one love," Nic declared.

With a tender nudge, Nic pushed her shoulders with his fingertips, causing her to fall back on the mattress. Aminah giggled, scooting further up the bed while watching him crawl towards her like a feral beast. He raised her right leg, kissing against her calf then gliding the tips of his nose against her skin.

"Ahh," Aminah moaned.

He hadn't done a thing and she was already approaching climax. Her body betrayed her efforts to fake like she hadn't craved this man. She was uncertain of what was to come once he kissed her kitty. *Mass destruction,* she thought.

"I smell you, Love. And you smell so fucking good," Nic growled.

Yep. I'm a goner, Aminah mused.

Nic delighted in her aroma, now it was time for him to feast. Drizzling soft kisses against the smooth, plump skin encasing her clit, he hesitated for a second too long and Aminah was anxious.

"What happened? What's wrong?" she huffed, longing for a dozen more of his tiny kisses.

Nic shook his head. His eyes were heavy with something that Aminah could not decipher.

Fear? No. The fire in his eyes wreaked with eagerness.

Worry. Maybe. Uncertainty dripped from Nic and Aminah's relationship, but they would stink with discombobulation after sharing in this.

She eyed him once more. Pure, unadulterated longing ladened his dark eyes.

He shook his head again.

"Nothing, Love. I just like to take a moment to admire the beauty of new places before I explore."

Aminah didn't have a second to respond. Nic blanketed her essence with his mouth. He sucked and slurped in slow unhasty circles, allowing his tongue to gradually take root in her center.

"Oh my. Oh my god," Aminah whined, clutching handfuls of her hair.

She gazed down at Nic in disbelief, requiring a visual of his tongue lashing. With closed eyes, he tongue-kissed her pussy lips with relentless persistence. Each lick, each kiss, every moan from his lungs was a calculated tease intentionally designed to drive her insane.

"Nic. Nicolas. No... no. Yes. Shit," she bellowed.

"Mmhmm," he hummed, pressing both hands against her hips to control her gyrations.

"Can I have you, Aminah? Let me in. Whatever is broken, let me fix it."

Aminah stroked his face, eyes lingering to memorize the strong lines of his jaw, the deep arch of his brows, and the cute way his nose wrinkled when he smiled. She took a lengthy moment to store each detail away for safekeeping.

Kissing her softly was momentary. Intense expectancy transformed the tenderness to a beautiful battering. Their tongues partnered, dancing to the most beautiful music. Hesitantly, Nic pulled away from her luscious lips, allowing his tongue to explore her neck.

Aminah was always in her head, always talking herself out of *this*. Nic's approach was unhurried and delicate; careful and deliberate with his words and every advance.

Eyes locked passionately, Nic kissed her nose as he entered her oasis. A bolt of lightning broke through her middle. Her eyes watered, not from the pain, but the warmth and security his embraced provided.

With every sweet hug and gentle caress, Nic unlocked a hidden reservoir that stored all of her secrets... *except for one.*

"Aminah. My god. You're more perfect than I imagined," Nic whimpered.

"Ahh. Ahh. Ahh," Aminah panted, unable to formulate a coherent retort.

"Come with me, Love," he moaned.

"Yes. Nic. Yes."

The room was flooded with the soft glow of moonlight and the hum of his quiet breathing. Nic was sound asleep, sprawled across the bed on his stomach. Aminah glanced at her phone, time seemingly moving at warp speed. Syncere would be arriving to pick her up in a few hours. Exhaustion crept in, betraying her desire to simply watch him. Viewing her phone one last time, she set the alarm to buzz on her Apple watch. Finally surrendering to sleep, she nestled into Nic. Instinctively, he kissed her temple as their limbs tangled.

"Goodnight, Love," he mumbled groggily, still fast asleep.

"Goodbye," she whispered.

The early morning sun bathed the loft in its warm embrace. Nic squinted, regretting that he'd been putting off getting curtains for the oversized windows. He reached across the bed, prepared to pull the covers over Aminah to protect her from the beaming rays, but the bed was empty.

His brow furrowed as his eyes quickly surveyed the open space: the satin dress thrown across the chair in the corner was gone, her glasses she put on in the middle of the night after discarding her contacts were missing from the side table. The bathroom door was open but dark, and the kitchen was empty. All traces of his lovie were gone.

What the fuck? He mouthed, dragging a hand down his face as he lifted in the bed.

Nic knew it would be in vain, but he spoke her name anyway.

"Lovie. Aminah."

Nothing. Silence.

Shifting his naked frame, he retrieved his phone from the nightstand. There were no text messages or calls. Nic didn't want to call Symphony the morning after her wedding, and he hated to call Syncere this early, but he needed to find Aminah. He opted to call King instead.

"What up, bro?" King answered, clearing his throat.

"Aye, is Aminah over there?" Nic blurted, skipping the niceties.

"Nah. Syncere took her to the airport a couple hours ago. She was picking her up from your place this morning," King explained.

"Airport… for what?"

"Man, you should call Syncere because I don't really know. She said Aminah was traveling for work or something. I was drunk as hell last night so I don't remember much of the conversation."

"Alright, man. I'll call you back."

Fuck. Nic shouted while dialing Syncere.

"Hello," she sang.

"Hey, Syn. Why did you take Aminah to the airport this morning?" he interrogated a bit harsher than intended.

"Um, what do you mean? She's on her way to London."

"London!" he shouted questioningly. "For what?"

"Yeah. London. She accepted a four-month professorship at a university there. An art history intensive program for grad students. You didn't know," Syncere uttered her last sentence as more of a statement than a question.

Nic shook his head as if Syncere could see him.

"Nah, sis. I didn't know shit," Nic muttered. Defeat lacing his tone.

"Nic, just call her. I'm sure she can expl-" Syncere tried, but Nic quickly interrupted.

"Nah, Syncere. This wasn't something she just decided," he said.

"But Nic -"

"When you talk to her... Give Aminah my best, alright."

He shook his head.

"I'm done."

6

FOUR MONTHS LATER

"Kai, that tickles." She whined, twirling the two carat engagement ring as she aimlessly gazed into the beautiful setting sun.

Aminah and Malakai were lovingly entangled as they nestled in the hammock on the house's porch. The beautiful domicile had three bedrooms and bathrooms, a large great room, a gorgeous kitchen, and a massive wraparound porch. It was perfect for a quick weekend getaway for two busy graduate students and the ideal home to buy as a surprise during Malakai's proposal to his girlfriend.

"I love you, Kai." Aminah hummed.

"I love you, Peanut." Malakai planted a soft kiss against her temple.

"Are you sure about this, bae?" she uttered, gazing at the sparkling diamond.

"I've never been more certain about anything in my life, Aminah. I love you with everything in me. I want to spend the rest of my days loving you. You are my dream come true, baby. Tell me you'll love me forever, Mi."

. . .

"We will be making our final descent into St. Louis. Flight attendants, please prepare for landing."

Aminah audibly gasped, stirred from her dream by the screech of the pilot's voice over the intercom. She nervously peered around, wiping the corners of her mouth as she began to recognize her surroundings. Glancing at her watch, Aminah quickly realized that she'd slept most of the eleven hour flight from London.

She'd spent the last four months engulfed in intensive creative writing courses as a visiting professor at Birkbeck, University of London. Aminah and a select group of Monroe University students were selected to participate in the semester abroad.

She'd known about the opportunity for several weeks before she decided to go. Even the night her and Nicolas's relationship elevated to another level: a sexual level. *Dare I say, lovemaking,* she thought. After that man made her body experience feelings that had laid dormant for years, Aminah practically sprinted out of his house in the middle of the night. The way Nic caressed her in his sleep as if he had no intentions of relinquishing her from his hold or heart, she knew she had to go. Evacuate immediately.

Thirty minutes later, Aminah exited the plane and trekked through the busy airport to retrieve her baggage. Checking her watch, she called Symphony for the third time since she didn't respond to the text informing her that she'd landed.

"Welcome back, babe," voices boomed from across the airport.

Her beam was as wide as a highway at the sound of the giggly squeals attached to the faces of her two best friends. Symphony's big honey blonde curls stood out in any crowd. Her tall curvy frame in skin tight jeans and thigh high boots held no evidence of a four month old baby at home.

Syncere's frame wrapped in milk chocolate skin was just as stately. Her growing baby bump was evident in the fitted cable knit sweater dress and heeled boots that Aminah was certain did not have King's approval. They hurriedly closed the small gap between them and embraced in a sisterly hug.

"Y'all act like I'm returning from war or something," Aminah joked.

"Well, it may as well have been war since we've only talked to you maybe three times in four months," Symphony fussed.

"I told y'all, I was self-"

"Reflecting. We know bitch. That was your response every time either of us texted or called you." Symphony rolled her eyes and pulled her friend in for another hug.

"Seriously, Minah. Are you good?" Syncere asked, resting gentle hands on her friend's shoulders. Her expression mirrored the meaning of her name.

Aminah nodded before releasing a deep sigh.

"Yeah. I will be. I've made some decisions. They won't be easy but they're necessary."

Syncere and Symphony nodded in understanding as they relieved their sisterfriend of some of her bags. Exiting the airport, Aminah shook her head at the sight of Symphony's SUV illegally parked in the passenger pickup zone.

"Backup. Backup. We're here," Symphony barked while waving her hand, shooing off the security guard.

"Shorty, you lucky y'all out here looking like Destiny's Child. I would give you a ticket if y'all was ugly," the guard said, proudly flashing his rusted gold grills.

With matching looks of disgust, the trio simultaneously mumbled, "Thanks."

Symphony navigated the streets of St. Louis on a chilly, yet gorgeous sunny day. It was one of those perfect winter days and Aminah was pleased to be back home. Well, her new home. Aminah had lived in Monroe City most of her adult life but St. Louis was home. She'd grown up in a suburb of the city before attending college a couple of hours away. Returning would be bittersweet for more reasons than anyone would ever know.

Aminah decided to move permanently to Haven Pointe after carefully considering an opportunity with the newly developed Monroe University Arts and Culture Foundation. The four months spent in London confirmed that being in the classroom no longer sparked excitement for her. Leading the vision and strategy for the foundation was the opportunity of a lifetime—a fresh start.

"Sooo... have you -" Aminah started but was quickly interrupted by her friends who simultaneously uttered...

"Nope."

"Y'all don't even know what I was about to ask," Aminah said, rolling her eyes.

"Minah, we've only known you for over fifteen years," Syncere voiced over her shoulder from the front passenger seat.

"Which means we know you have been itching to ask us about Nic," Symphony continued.

There was an awkward moment of silence as Symphony and Syncere focused on the road while Aminah bore her eyes into the sides of their faces from the back seat.

"Well," Aminah yelped.

Syncere chuckled while hesitantly mumbling, "Well, Nic is

doing pretty good. He's been busy with his new place and the winery."

"And Fallon," Symphony matter-of-factly said in her unapologetic way.

The silence was back but deafening and thorny this time, pricking Aminah right in the heart. *Fallon. He's back with his ex.*

"Prima!" Syncere yelled, pushing her cousin in the arm.

"Minah knows I am always going to give it to her raw and real," Symphony directed her comment to her cousin, before darting her eyes to the rearview mirror, peering at Aminah's reflection.

"We've seen them out only a few times since you've been gone," she continued, softening her approach.

Symphony muttered some other words but her tenor was white noise to Aminah. She plopped her head back, recalling the last voice message she received from Nic.

"Lovie, I'm at a loss right now. Syn and Symphony keep reassuring me that you're ok and you need time, but I really thought we were better than this. At a minimum, I thought we were friends, Aminah. But friends don't do this shit to each other. I hope you're good and taking care of whatever it is that caused you to run out on me. This is it for me, Love. Be good to yourself."

There were at least twenty messages before that, but Nicolas never ended them that way. Never a finale. But that message was the last time she'd heard from him... eight weeks ago. Just enough time to be *exclusive* or whatever with... Fallon. *Of all the women in the world, he would go back to her.* Aminah mused as she opened her eyes, noticing they'd pulled into Syncere's driveway.

The oversized door to the mini-mansion they lovingly nicknamed *Cartwright Castle* opened, and two miniature versions of Syncere and King came darting out. Empress and King Elias were their three-year-old twins and the cutest little humans Aminah had ever seen.

"Mimi. Mimi," the twins sang, tackling Aminah's legs.

"How are my favorite two year old twins?" she bantered, kneeling to embrace them.

"No, not two, Mimi-" King Elias started before his sister interrupted.

"We are three," Empress squealed with three tiny fingers boldly lifted.

"It's me and Eli's birthday," she matter-of-factly continued.

"Ok, little munchkins, it's time to get ready for your party," King chuckled, ushering the kids towards the house.

He stretched his arms to pull Aminah into a hug.

"Good to see you, sis. You've been missed... by everybody." King winked, playfully pinching her cheek.

"I guess we'll see if that's true, huh, bro?" Aminah mumbled, uncertain if everybody truly missed her.

Once again, Syncere outdid herself for the twin's birthday. A gang of rambunctious kids enjoyed the Busy Bee-themed party until they practically passed out in the basement of the Cartwright home.

"This is why TJ and True will have parties at Chuck E Cheese or somewhere other than my house. Look at all of this shit," she fussed, glancing around at the mess.

The bouncing baby in her arms cooed in agreement with her mommy. Just a couple of weeks after their wedding, Symphony and Tyus welcomed a seven-pound-ten-ounce baby girl named True Syncere Okoro.

Syncere, Symphony, and Aminah settled on the couch, staring at plates of half-eaten cake, empty juice boxes, and trash splayed across the dark walnut floor. The house was now clear of sugar-induced cackling kids and exhausted parents but they'd left a mess.

"That's why you pay a cleaning crew. They will be here momentarily," Syncere said, rolling her eyes at her cousin as she kicked up her swollen feet on the ottoman.

Quiet, mixed with sleepiness hovered over them.

"Minah, why don't you go get some rest? I'm sure you're exhausted and jet-lagged," Syncere offered.

"That... And she's wondering where the handsome Nicolas Touissant was this evening," Symphony blurted.

Aminah rolled her eyes.

"Why does everything come back to Nic for you?" Aminah probed irritably.

"Speak for yourself, sis. Make me believe that you weren't holding your breath every time someone strolled down those steps," Symphony said, pursing her lips awaiting Aminah's vain attempt to convince her otherwise.

"Shut up," Aminah muttered, but she couldn't contain her giggle.

Symphony was right. Every time the steps creaked her eyes darted to the open-staircase in search of *him.* It wasn't until the twins opened their gifts that she realized Nic wasn't coming.

"This is from Uncle Nic," King said, handing two large gift bags to the twins. "He's out of town and sad he missed your party."

Immediately, Aminah's mind shifted to Fallon. *Did he take her somewhere? A romantic weekend getaway perhaps?*

Aminah had never met Fallon but knew she could potentially present a problem since Nic was a critical part of her *fresh start.*

"Are they back together?" she blurted, pulling her friends from a conversation she'd neglected to follow.

Matching gray eyes glanced at each other and then over to their friend.

"Nic and Fallon?" Syncere said, shaking her head.

Aminah nodded.

"No... I don't think so. No..." Syncere stressed the last word.

The room was hushed again, but the elephant lingering in the space was loud.

"But can I ask you a question?" Syncere raised a brow.

Aminah nodded.

"What can you say or do if they were?"

Aminah's brown eyes shimmered with sadness... regret.

Nothing. She thought but would dare let the words see the light of day.

"Minah, you left that man with no explanation... not even a goodbye," Syncere uttered.

"*After* fucking him," Symphony chimed. "Let's not forget that important fact. Not even a *Dear John* text."

"You were wrong, Mi. And he deserves an apology," her friends almost uttered in unison.

Aminah nodded.

The glistening pools of unshed tears betrayed her attempt to appear unruffled.

7

Aminah was awakened by the boisterous sounds of toddlers fighting over their new toys. She stayed at Syncere's house until her condo would be ready in a few weeks. Aminah had the option of staying with her parents but they lived too far from the action in Haven.

Thinking of her parents, Aminah reached for her cell phone to call them since they got in late from a vacation. Aaron and Desirae Loveless were living their best lives at fifty-seven years old. After selling a small chain of specialty grocery stores across Missouri to a larger chain over five years ago, her parents vowed to live a carefree life since they'd smartly invested their money.

"Minah," her dad sang.

She shook her head because he never said *hello* when she called. He'd simply speak her name and wait for his daughter to say something.

"Hey, Dad," Aminah cooed, smiling at the mere sound of his velvety voice.

"Hey, sugarlump. When am I going to lay my eyes on my second favorite girl?"

"I'm never going to make it to number one, huh?" she teased.

"Nope. Not until I'm dead and gone," her mother shouted in the background which meant that Aminah was on speaker phone.

"Dad, you really should tell people when they're on speaker phone," Aminah fussed.

"It's my phone and I'll do what I want," he bantered.

She shook her head.

"Hi, Ma."

"Hi, beautiful. I can't wait to see you tonight," her mother uttered.

Aminah's parents were attending tonight's grand opening and fundraising gala at the Cartwright Innovation Center. King and Syncere had worked tirelessly for the past few years to open the center and the day was finally here. The center wouldn't fully open to the public for another few weeks, but tonight was the soft opening.

"Me too."

"Have you talked to Nicolas?" Mrs. Loveless asked.

"Ma," Aminah whined.

"What? It was just a question."

"No, Ma. I have not talked to Nic."

Mrs. Loveless shook her head.

"You know I am going to always tell you the truth. And this time, honey, you were wrong. Nic was your friend and he deserved better from you," her mother fussed.

Aminah's body jerked, her mother's words were like bullets riddling her heart. She was about to provide a lame explanation but then heard her mother's voice echoing, *'Here. Talk to your daughter.'*

“Baby girl, don’t mind your mother. But she’s not wrong, Mi,” Mr. Loveless said.

“I know, Daddy. Nobody knows how wrong I was more than me,” she paused, taking a few deep breaths. “I gotta go. I see you all tonight.”

Aminah fell back on the bed contemplating her parents' words. They adored Nic and thought that he was perfect for her, but they did not understand the demons she wrestled.

"Minah, we’re leaving in five minutes,” Syncere said from the other side of the bedroom door.

Rolling her eyes, she rushed into the bathroom to freshen up. Still, she secretly wished she could nestle back into the comfortable king size bed and hibernate for the foreseeable future.

“Damn, Mi... you out here like Patti Patti with a new attitude,” Syncere snapped her fingers. “You look amazing, friend.”

Aminah smirked, trying her best not to laugh. Staring at her reflection in the compact mirror, Aminah slightly regretted instructing her stylist, Deeny, to ‘*chop it all off.’* For as long as she could remember, *Minah with the long curly hair* was how everyone described her. Now, she was Minah with the funky asymmetrical bob cut that allowed her natural big curls to flourish. One side was cut low, while the other side had bouncy tresses draped across her eye.

“Aminah Rae, stop it. You look hot, bitch,” Symphony squealed. Snapping her fingers for emphasis.

Snapping the mirror closed, Aminah playfully rolled her eyes at her silly friend. They all looked amazing. King had arranged for car service to pick them up for the big night. The Cartwright Innovation Center’s opening gala was Haven's most talked about event.

The Cartwright's had already hosted a ribbon cutting ceremony earlier in the week for the community. Still, tonight was an opportunity for them to connect with local partners and secure additional donations.

A few years ago when King purchased the lot that had been vacant for years, he dreamed of a place where kids in the community could go after school and during the summers. His wife, Syncere, expanded his idea into an innovation center for young kids to develop and entrepreneurs to thrive.

The crew, minus Nicolas, was piled in the Escalade limousine heading to the event. Approaching the center, everyone's faces brightened at the sight of the flashing lights and red carpet leading to the front door. The media and photographers shoved their microphones and cameras into the faces of the attendees, who included all of the business owners in Haven, CEOs and Presidents of corporations, and local celebrities.

King and Syncere stepped out of the limousine. Their eyes pranced around, landing on the massive marquee carrying their family's name. Clutching her hand in his, King gazed down at his wife. Syncere was gorgeous in a sparkling silver strapless gown that reflected against her gray eyes. He kissed against her temple, then a delicate peck to her glossed lips.

"I'm so proud of you, husband," Syncere whispered with pride and excitement.

"I'm proud of you, wife. Thank you for believing in me, Princess. When a lot of people thought I was crazy, you trusted me to finish this. Thank you, baby," King uttered with much gratitude, getting a little choked up.

The Cartwright's stood at the end of the red carpet, intimately connected as if they were the only people in the world. Cameras and flashing lights couldn't interfere with their moment.

After one final kiss, they turned to face the crowd and quickly transitioned to the power couple of Haven Pointe.

Over one hundred people filled the modern-decorated, high-tech center. The gym had been transformed into an upscale, glamorous space. Black silk draped the walls, sequin rose-gold cloths covered the tables and servers outfitted in black and white tuxedos passed champagne flutes to guests. The gala featured services and products from local, minority-owned businesses, while high-end donated items were displayed for the silent auction.

"You ready to exceed our goal tonight, boss lady?" Elori said, smiling at Syncere.

"Yes ma'am. You did an amazing job. Expect a big bonus... *boss lady,*" Syncere teased.

Elori Maxey was the center's newly hired director. She was responsible for everything from managing staff to organizing all activities, including the gala.

"Elori, this is my best friend, Aminah Loveless. Aminah, this is Elori Maxey, our director of *everything,*" Syncere laughed.

"Nice to meet you. This is outstanding. My friend here is hard to please so you make sure she gets you that bonus," Aminah said, taking a sip of champagne.

When she saw her parents walk in, her smile widened, and her lips were still connected to the glass flute. Aminah shook her head because her parents were downright gorgeous, dressed in all black. After all of these years, they still turned heads.

"Hey, sexy lady," Aminah squealed, causing her mother to spin around.

"My beautiful baby girl. Look at you," her mother tittered, clasping Aminah's cheeks in the palms of her hands.

"Unhand the girl, Desirae. It's my turn," her father playfully demanded.

"Daddy," Aminah yelped, falling into the comforting arms of her first love.

Sensing that she needed his familiar embrace, Mr. Loveless held onto his daughter a little longer, squeezed a bit tighter. Mrs. Loveless watched them, her heart filled with gratitude and glumness. Grateful that Aminah had a father who was the perfect model of a good man and saddened because the shadow of grief and regret overcast her soul. It dimmed her light, darkening the whites of her beautiful brown eyes.

"You cut your hair," Desirae declared, interrupting the daddy-daughter time.

Mr. Loveless released his daughter right after placing one more kiss on her forehead. Aminah swiped a stray curl and ran her fingers through the cropped tresses.

"Do you like it?" she asked, nervously.

"I love it," her mother answered, fingering soft curls.

"I thought you would be mad because I cut my *crowning glory*," Aminah quipped, mocking her grandmother's words about her hair.

"You've been listening to your Grandma Glory too much," Desirae smirked, thinking about her mother's often antiquated opinions.

"Now I love my mother dearly, but that old woman is wrong a lot," Desirae laughed.

Stepping closer to her daughter, she cupped her chin with one hand, while fixing the strap of her dress with the other.

"Aminah Rae, your hair is not your crown. That strength lives here," she said, pointing to Aminah's head. "...and here." Desirae concluded, pointing to her daughter's heart.

Aminah nodded.

"I'm gonna to tell GG, you called her an old woman," she giggled, hugging her mother.

Still pressed against her ear, Desirae whispered, "Sweetheart, did you find what you needed during this break to help you heal?"

"Almost, Ma. Almost."

"Well, you better act fast," Mrs. Lovelace said as she pulled away.

Aminah followed her mother's eyes and they landed on a caramel-dipped, stocky, hunk of human flesh. *Nic.*

There he was, and he was... *beautiful.* The black tuxedo was nothing more than an accessory on him. Nic looked good in anything. Even those ugly oversized plastic pants he wore when working in the vineyard. But Aminah had to admit, he'd aged like fine wine in the past four months. He'd cut his short coils into a low Caesar-fade, now complemented with a shadowy beard. Diamond studs glistened in both ears, but his hazel eyes always dampened her panties.

Aminah cleared her throat, unsuccessfully trying to remove the lump that formed. Snagging a glass of champagne from a passing tray, she downed the bubbly in one gulp. Her parents dashed off to dance, while her Jimmy Choo's were bolted to the floor. With her mouth wide opened, she looked around the room trying to find an escape. Aminah wanted to melt. Vanish so that she would not have to face him. And *her.*

The rathole known as Facebook had allowed Aminah to become familiar with Fallon's face. Butterscotch skin and chocolate brown eyes were the highlights of her pretty face. Aminah hated that this woman was wearing the hell out of a crimson-colored fitted sequin dress.

She stared at the pair, focused on Fallon's arm entwined with Nic's. She laughed and talked with King and Tyus with so much familiarity... comfort. *Those are my people. My friends.* She pondered loudly.

"I have to get out of here," she breathed to nobody but herself before darting towards the restroom.

The fellas exchanged daps and pleasantries while King pulled Nic to the side. Fallon had excused herself so it was the perfect time to inform... shit, *warn* Nic of Aminah's return.

"Hey, man, um... Aminah's back," King announced.

Nic's expression was unperturbed but his insides were all topsy-turvy.

"When?" he asked cooly.

"A few days ago. Before the twin's birthday party."

Nic nodded.

"Good for her. I hope she's well."

"That's it?" King uttered curiously.

Nic nodded again.

"That's all. Aminah made her choice. And it's clear that the shit don't include me," he said, a hint of dismay quivered his voice.

"Man... Nic. You can't tell me that you don't love that girl."

"Nah. I can never tell you that, bro, because I love the shit out of that woman. But I'm done with the chase. Even if she would never be mine like I want, I at least thought we were friends. And friends don't do the shit that Aminah did."

Nic hadn't told King, or anybody, that he and Aminah had sex the night before she left. Those details were personal; a topic for him and his lovie to dissect. But Nic honestly was unsure if he could even revisit that night.

He would never forget, but every second of the past four months was needed to gradually tuck away the memory of her skin enmeshed with his. Aminah would always linger in the recesses of his mind like a buried treasure waiting to be unearthed. But Nic was determined to keep his hurt and angst concealed from the world—from *her.*

King patted his friend on the shoulder as they walked to the bar. Nic needed a drink. A strong one. Anger and anticipation caused the hair on his arms to stand at attention. He desperately desired to see her face, but the lingering resentment was potent.

"Hey, handsome," a voice chimed.

Nic jumped, shaken from his dazed state.

"Hey," he responded to Fallon. "You good?"

She nodded.

"Just had to visit the ladies room," she said then paused for a heartbeat.

"I, um, didn't realize Aminah was back. Have you two had a chance to catch up?" Fallon inquired.

"No. We haven't,' Nic said blandly.

His response was short and his guise told her not to probe further.

Nic and Fallon's reacquaintance was recent, and their past was complicated. Nic met Fallon Burris ten years ago through mutual friends when he lived in New York. Nic was recently discharged from the Air Force and was living his best life traveling the world. He settled on the East Coast for a while when he was offered a leadership role in sales for a liquor distribution company.

Fallon worked at the same company and was from O'Fallon, Illinois, about thirty minutes across the bridge dividing Missouri and Illinois. They immediately found common ground through their profession and Midwest connection.

What started as merely a physical relationship became years of dating that *almost* led to a proposal. But when Nic's father suddenly died, his plans to live the power couple life in NYC died too. While Fallon was sympathetic about his dad's passing, she did not understand him moving to Brighton to run his family's winery. In her words, *"I don't give a fuck about tradition. What about me?"*

After many years of no communication, Fallon saw a post on social media about Nic's new business adventure. She reached out because she was still working in the liquor distribution business but in Chicago. Her message popped up in his DMs just days after Aminah left.

Nic did not answer for weeks because he was well aware of the complications that Fallon presented. But when he ran into a few snags with his liquor licensing, he responded. *There was no backsliding, just business,* he thought. Fallon had been extremely instrumental in helping him navigate hurdles with his bar, but she was hushed about her desire to *navigate* him.

Fallon had recently broken up with her ex, Scott, and Nic wasn't sure how to define the end of his relationship with Aminah, so the former lovers found new *friendship* in each other.

Deciding not to press Nic about Aminah's return, she sipped her wine and turned her focus to the stage when Elori, the center's director, tapped on the microphone, attempting to gain the crowd's attention.

"Hello. Hello, everyone," Elori sang.

The partygoers began to simmer and move a bit closer to the stage.

"Thank you all so much for supporting tonight's event. It has truly been a labor of love for the entire CIC team," she said, motioning her hand towards a group of people who worked for the center.

The crowd clapped in recognition.

"Now, I would like to bring to the stage one of the most

dynamic, loving power couples I've ever met. Without their vision, none of this would be possible. Please give a round of applause for Mr. and Mrs. Cartwright."

Resounding ovations and cheers echoed through the space. Hand-in-hand, King and Syncere sauntered towards the stage.

"Thank you so much, Elori. None of this would be possible without *you,*" King stressed, causing another round of clapping.

"A few years ago, this piece of land was completely empty. I remember the night I brought Syncere here and she looked at me like I was crazy," he laughed, looking at his wife as she nodded.

"I told her that I wanted to erect a foundation for the community. Both Haven Pointe and Grover Heights. To have a place where all kids... *My kids...* can learn, grow, and create. The Cartwright Innovation Center will offer sports programs, technology classes, incubation space for future entrepreneurs, and so much more." King paused to accept the bravos.

"I want to thank my beautiful wife, Syncere, for believing in me. For rocking with me through the ups and downs of this project while raising two toddlers and nurturing another life," he uttered, placing a hand on her growing belly.

King kissed Syncere and whispered, *"I love you,"* for her ears only.

"We also want to thank our family and friends. Come on up y'all," Syncere said. "Prima, Tyus, Minah, Nic, come on."

Both King and Syncere waved their hands, encouraging their people to be recognized. Nic's eyes quickly danced through his group of friends searching for *her.* Aminah had watched his every move throughout the night so that she could hide away. When he moved, she moved in the opposite direction. But now that she was summoned by name, Aminah had no choice but to reveal herself.

Strolling through the crowd, Aminah approached the stage

and walked up the few steps to join her crew. Her eyes locked with Syncere's and Symphony's knowing gaze. Symphony winked then gestured for her friend to lift her head. The fire and earth to her wind would always adjust her crown when weak. Inhaling deeply, a closed mouth, yet genuine smile graced her face. Through an audible exhale, her stare collided with *his.*

Nicolas was speechless. He heard the crowd and saw the people, but when their eyes met, everything went *silent*—as if the room was constructed for just the two of them. At that moment, she was the only thing worth seeing.

She was magnificent. Time hadn't altered the allure of her pretty face now framed with short luscious curls. The black dress decorated her curves like luxurious silk. Every stitch and seam caressed her body with a gentle embrace. The draped one shoulder was flattering but the high side slit that accentuated one thick thigh was mesmerizing. Flashbacks of those thighs wrapped around his neck while he indulged in her essence had him adjusting his stance. *Fuck!*

Aminah's copper eyes were glazed with conflict. To onlookers, she was filled with happiness for her friends. But she knew... *He knew* a silent struggle circled like a category five hurricane ready to wreak havoc. Like magnets, their stares were inevitably drawn to each other, yet dismayed by the force of conflicting emotions.

Apology secreted from her, while acrimony shrouded him. Their hearts were a battlefield where love and loathing waged war. Both vying for dominance, influence over the other's heart. With a sudden jolt, a wave of claps and whistles brought them back to the here and now. The greetings and speeches had ended and the party was back in full swing.

"Go talk to him, Minah," Syncere encouraged while whispering in her ear before exiting the stage.

Aminah nodded, following behind her friend. She could feel Nic's presence behind her. His scent wrapped around her like her favorite lover. Remembrance of his whisperings of sweet nothings in her ear as he plunged deeper into her core had her breathless and dizzy. Losing her balance on the last step, a gentle, yet firm hand clutched her arm. His touch shot a rush of warmth through her veins.

"Careful," he cautioned, as his fingertips brushed her velvet skin.

With every stroke, he left a trail of tingles that she'd favored more than she cared to confess.

Nic quickly released her arm. The need to run away was urgent. He was so damn mad, but so fucking happy to see her at the same time. A storm raged in his mind. Lightning flashes of memories of her in his bed followed by thunderous crashes of hurt. Nic was able to avoid the revelation until she was in his presence. His lovie. His friend... Broke him.

"Nic," she breathed, anxiousness leaking from her tone.

He heard her, but he kept walking.

"Nic, please," Aminah muttered, touching his back.

Like a wicked spell, his feet suddenly turned into boulders, her touch instantly paused his pursuit. Wrestling with how he would respond, Nic inhaled deeply to drain the tension from his body. But, being face-to-face, vexation was washed over him like a titanic wave, further disturbing his troubled soul.

"Hi," she greeted. Her voice was so small and deflated.

"Hello, Aminah," Nic greeted her but it wasn't welcoming.

She swallowed hard. Hearing *Aminah* leave his tongue was like shards of glass through her heart. She was his love. His lovie. *Who the hell is Aminah?* She contemplated but knew that shit sounded crazy.

"Can we talk?"

Nic leered at her. His golden brown orbs burned with fierce intensity. Despite his best effort to erase the memories... to erase her—her pretty face and pouty lips were constant reminders of the love he carried for this woman.

"Please, Nic."

Her voice was a bittersweet echo cluttering the corners of his mind. Two halves of a broken mirror reflected each other's pain for unknown and unspoken reasons. Unbeknownst to them, their friends anxiously observed the exchange, hoping they could mend the shattered pieces.

Nic shook his head.

"No, Aminah. Maybe at some point, but not now." Nic shook his head, then turned and walked away.

Aminah gasped, feeling those shards of glass again. His departure cut deep. It felt like her body and mind were riddled with wounds that refused to heal.

8

Exactly six hundred and seventy-two hours have ticked by since the gala. A month ago and it felt like an eternity. Aminah's gorgeous face had kidnapped Nic's psyche and he could not loosen the shackles. She was driving him crazy. He couldn't focus and lacked motivation to do much of anything.

Deciding to get some shit done today, he'd been up since six in the morning for an intense hour-long workout with his trainer, managed inventory, and worked with the contractors to ensure all of the details for the grand opening were settled. It was after six o'clock in the evening and Nic was ready to call it quits and have a drink. The bell chimed when King walked through the door of the bar.

"What up. What up," King said, engaging in a gentleman's handshake with his friend.

He circled his eyes around the establishment and nodded.

"It's coming together, bro. How long?"

"Another month or so. The special plumbing for the bar is

almost done. But once the liquor license is clear, I can breathe a lil bit. The rules for bourbon are drastically different from serving wine only. A few hiccups but I'm back on track."

"Is that Fallon's doing?" King asked, eyeing Nic curiously.

"Some of the things. Yeah. She's definitely the reason why the license is being expedited."

"So, what's up with y'all?" King interrogated.

"We're just chilling. No strings. No commitments. No expectations," Nic declared, filling two glasses with the dark liquor.

"Hey. Hey," a baritone voice echoed.

Tyus strolled in, surprising his friends.

"I thought you had TJ tonight," Nic asked.

"Man, TJ be ghosting me… My own son plays me on the regular," Tyus chuckled.

"Anytime he can hang with his baby sister, dear old Dad is an afterthought," he laughed. "My mom gave Symphony a little break and picked up True. TJ hopped in the car, too."

They cackled because their friend truly looked brokenhearted. Nic poured a third glass and then rounded the bar to join his friends at the round walnut table. He audibly sighed and plopped down in the plush deep green leather chair.

"So back to Fallon," King uttered, resuming their previous conversation. "No strings but y'all fucking?" he said questioningly.

"We fucked. Once. It wasn't my best moment but it happened. It was more about familiarity and nothing else. Not an excuse but it's the truth. Fallon knows what it is with us."

"So what does that mean for you and Aminah? What is it with y'all?" Tyus asked.

Nic's eyes narrowed to slits, tossing his head back.

Sighing, he practically grunted the words.

"There is no me and Aminah. She made her choice so it ain't shit with us."

"Has she though? Seems to me she's looking to make a fresh start," King declared.

"How so?" Nic said.

"Moving to Haven for one, accepting that new job," Tyus said.

But he quickly realized he'd said too much when Nic's head craned in shock and confusion.

"Moving to Haven. When? Where? What job?" Nic blurted.

King and Tyus glanced at each other before planting their eyes back on Nic. King rubbed a distressed hand down his face. *Awe shit.*

"Um, Nic, man. You should go talk to her," King stuttered, trying to avert Nic's death glare.

"Y'all niggas acting like some lil girls now? Keeping secrets and shit," Nic argued.

"It's not our business to tell," King declared.

"Fuck it," Tyus barked. "Aminah's renting Syncere's old condo. She moved in on Sunday."

Nic shook his head in disbelief. He couldn't do anything but snicker but the scowl lacing his face indicated anger. He tried to suppress the feelings, but vexation pulsed through his veins like an unstoppable runaway train.

"So she's down the fucking street. That's what you're saying," Nic shouted, pointing a rigid finger toward the building that was less than a mile away.

King and Tyus nodded simultaneously.

"Symphony mentioned something about her running the university foundation now. They opened an office in the city," Tyus added.

Wow, Nic mouthed. This whole conversation had him questioning the past years of his friendship with Aminah.

"It's clear to me that there's no point in talking to Aminah. We aren't friends like I thought. First, she leaves with no word for months, then her lil ass blows back in town like nothing has happened. Now, she lives down the fucking street from me and I didn't even know," Nic barked, tossing back his drink before slamming the glass on the table.

"Didn't she try to talk to you at the gala?" Tyus egged, shrugging dismissively.

King shook his head because Tyus was adding gallons of fuel to what was right now a small, manageable fire.

"You wasn't fucking with her that night. Maybe she wanted to share all of this then," Tyus continued, pouring it on even thicker.

Nic's leer was a fiery inferno ready to light up his friend. King lowered his head slowly, begging Tyus to shut the hell up.

"So... this shit is my fault?" Nic probed, before shooting straight up from his chair.

"You know what, man. Never mind. I don't want to talk about shit pertaining to Aminah Loveless anymore," he said, ending the chatter.

He darted his eyes from King to Tyus, daring them to say another word. Seeing none, he hurriedly crossed the room to pour himself another drink. Another hour passed as the guys shot the shit and watched random sports podcasts.

Nic stared blankly at the television while Aminah trespassed through his mind. The door chimed again when their friend Lennox came by to deliver a sample of specialty cigars Nic was considering retailing at the bar.

"I ain't never seen this nigga drunk like this," Lennox whispered to King as they both watched Nic down another bourbon.

King shook his head.

"Man, he's messed up about Aminah. I don't know what happened before she left, but she fucked my mans up."

"He needs to talk to her. We're too grown to be making shit up in our heads," Tyus said, keeping his voice low.

"Fuck that," Lennox whisper-yelled. "*She's* the one that has some explaining to do."

"Real shit," King agreed, lifting his glass in agreement.

Nic was still facing the television while his crew was across the space leaning against the bar. They stared at him with real concern for their friend. Nic was as calm and collected as they came so for him to be ruffled was uncommon. A sudden swarm of silence covered the room.

"Y'all niggas finished gossiping like some lil girls?" Nic slurred.

"Aye man, let's get you upstairs. I need to get home anyway," King insisted, patting Nic on the shoulder.

"I don't need no damn babysitter, bro," Nic complained.

"Understood, but you need to lock up and sleep this shit off, dawg," King continued.

Standing to his feet, Nic nodded before taking the last sip from his glass.

"I'm good, King. I'm cool. I'm going to wrap up a few things and then head upstairs."

The guys looked at him, seemingly to confirm that he was *cool.* Since Nic's apartment was above the bar, his friends felt comfortable leaving. After exchanging manly handshakes and daps, Nic locked the door. He washed the cognac glasses and turned off the televisions.

Wiping down the bar, his hand crashed into the box he'd been avoiding all day. A shipment of the new wine was delivered earlier but Nic refused to open the crate because too many memories... Hopes for the future were attached to the bottles inside.

Nic inhaled a deep breath to stave off the nausea building in his stomach. He wasn't sure if it was the alcohol or the recollections of the time he spent with Aminah at the winery. The day he designed the specialty wine especially for her.

Carefully, he cut open to the top of the box and peeled back each flap. Scooping handfuls of foam chips onto the bar top, he lifted one of the most exquisite bottles he'd ever seen. Nic swallowed hard at the site of the silver firefly flanking the top of the coral-hued glass bottle. *The same color of her dress,* he mused.

The bottle was more like a carefully crafted piece of art, with beveled carvings of fireflies on the glass. The label featured a black-and-white pencil sketch of a woman dancing under a large tree surrounded by colorful fireflies.

"What kind of wine did I make tonight, Nic?" Aminah giggled.

Nic was seated at the piano while she perused vintage decor dressing the room. A silent observer, Nic's eyes followed her every motion like a predator stalking prey. Listlessly tickling the piano keys, he was captivated by the graceful sway of her movements.

"What would you like to make?" he asked, still gazing at her.

Aminah felt his eyes on her and the predatory intensity dispatched shivers down her spine. She sipped the wine he poured her to quell the thunder bursting through her essence.

"Um... Something sweet, with a little bubbly," she laughed and he smiled.

"Fruity... Almost like a sangria but with a little more kick." She winked, trailing a finger across the fireplace mantle.

Nic nodded, nibbling his bottom lip because she was perfection.

"I got it," she chirped.

He remained muted but raised his brows, encouraging her to continue.

"You could mix up a new batch of wine with a hint of your fancy bourbon," she said, animatedly flailing her hands as if she was mixing something.

This time Nic laughed out loud.

"You think it's that simple, huh," he chuckled.

She shook her head.

"No, but it's the best parts of your dad's dream and your dream," she revealed, biting her lip to suppress the blush blanketing her face.

Nic's stare was long and fierce. He fixated on her with an unwavering regard that left her feeling both exhilarated and vulnerable.

Nic instantly leaped off the piano bench and quickly depleted their distance. Cupping her face into the palms of his hands, his lips hovered over hers. One breath... One slight gesture and his tongue would part her pouty lips.

"What's your dream, Lovie?" Nic asked, pressing his forehead to hers.

"I - I just wanted to glow, be free, like the fireflies," Aminah uttered unflinchingly.

Nic gasped, jolting from the recollections when his phone buzzed against the bar top. Blinking rapidly, he read the text message from King asking if he was good. He shot back a quick response of, *Yeah.*

He was far from good. Nic was reeling. Unable to disconnect his glare from the gorgeous bottle, he grabbed it from the countertop and stormed out of the bar. Pausing to lock the door, he could have taken that second to rethink what his was about to do, but -

"I'm fucked up as it is. May as well get this over with," he whimpered lowly.

* * *

Aminah rested in the claw-foot bathtub after a grueling day. At five a.m., she was on the road heading to Monroe City to pack the last few boxes before the moving company arrived. Saying goodbye to her townhouse was tough but fulfilling. For the first time in a very long time, Aminah made a decision for herself, and it felt good.

Stepping out of the tub once the water had chilled, Aminah lathered her body with sunflower oil, went through her facial routine, and dressed in a tattered T-shirt and underwear. It wasn't late, but she was exhausted and starving.

Navigating the hallway and into the kitchen, she was excited and overwhelmed by the move. Excitement sparked the gleam in her eyes because she loved her new space. She was drained and overcome because there was so much to do in such little time. Aside from getting her place together, Aminah would be reporting to her new job in just a few weeks.

The sounds of Muni Long piped through the surround sound speakers wired throughout the space. Yet, another reason why she was in love. Aminah plated the chicken panini and pasta salad she had delivered from *Sliced and Diced* then untwisted the cap from the bottle of red wine. It was no Touissant Winery, but whatever DoorDash could deliver would do. She looked at the stack of boxes marked *kitchen* and groaned. The contents were a mystery and she had no clue where to find a wine glass.

"I guess I'm straight from the bottle with it," she cackled, carrying her items to the dining room table.

The iPad was charged and already set to Netflix. Aminah planned to watch a few episodes of *Survival of the Thickest* until her eyes were too heavy to function. With one leg tucked underneath her butt and the other leg resting in a chair, she sighed after the first bite of the flavorful sandwich.

Knock. Knock. Knock.

With a furrowed brow, Aminah stuffed another spoonful of salad into her mouth. *Who the hell is knocking on my door like that?*

The only people who knew that she was moving today were her parents, Syncere, and Symphony, and she'd talked to each of them already. Grabbing her phone from the table, her finger hovered over the emergency call button as she cautiously crept to the door.

BANG. BANG. BANG.

Startled, she gasped when more aggressive knocking ensued. *Just be quiet and maybe they'll just go away.*

Aminah held her breath as if that would aid in her silence. Sliding over the tiny peephole flap, her lung capacity depleted at the site of *him.* With his head hanging low, Nic had two hands pressed against the door. She didn't have to fully see his face to know it was him. He lifted one balled fist ready to continue his disruption when Aminah snatched open the door.

Nic lifted his head, revealing narrowed, disturbed eyes. His guise was inflamed with something that should have scared her. But fear and Nic could not even exist in the same sentence. She surveyed him. Dressed in shorts and a winery-branded t-shirt, he languidly swayed. The massive consumption of alcohol was finally taking its toll... Or maybe it was the vision of *her.*

Nic held what appeared to be a bottle of wine but smelled like a distillery. His gorgeous honey eyes were heavy-lidded and dilated, making her wonder how much he'd consumed. Her notions about this moment were battling between puzzlement and possibilities. *Maybe he's ready to talk? Maybe he'll forgive me?*

"Did our friendship mean anything to you? Was it a fucking joke?" Nic blurted. His tone was low but weighty.

Aminah vigorously shook her head no. She opened her mouth to answer him but Nic quickly cut her off.

"Was I just something to do to help you pass the time? Get over whatever it is you needed to get over," Nic muttered.

"No. Nic, no," Aminah attested.

In an instant, her emotional state had morphed from tranquil to flustered. Tears teetered on her lashes, threatening to break free. Nic was vulnerable... Broken, and she was to blame. Tension crackled between them like electric currents. With each gaze, a silent challenge dared the other to look away first, to admit defeat.

Only minutes had ticked by since Nic bombarded her threshold, but a lifetime of unspoken words hung heavy between them. Aminah scanned her reddened eyes over him. Nic's chiseled features, rugged charm and sparkling orbs were always a vision of masculine beauty. But the man before her was dejected. Defeat weakened the strength of his broad, stately physique.

"Nic, our friendship meant everything. It *means* everything. Please, Nic, come in. Let me explain," she begged, reaching to touch his arm.

He yanked away from her as if her touch was deadly.

"It means everything but you left," Nic barked questioningly.

"Fucked me, then ghosted me like what we shared wasn't shit."

"I - I'm sorry. I'm so sorry," she choked out every word.

"I messed up and there are no excuses. Please, Nic. I am so sorry," Aminah groveled, feeling guilty and remorseful for her actions.

Her voice was barely audible above the sound of her heartbeat. A wail of a cry began to bubble in her chest. Aminah knew that her actions were wrong, but it wasn't until *that* moment when she realized the depth of the hurt she caused. Tears gradually flooded her face as she struggled to articulate her sorrow and regret.

"You have been the best friend to me even when I didn't deserve it. Leaving was wrong and my actions were selfish. But..."

Nic's lowered eyes quickly glanced at her. His stare permitted her to continue but warned her to proceed with caution.

"I was scared. That night at your house when you asked me to make a decision about us and I couldn't, I figured you were done with this... done with me. The opportunity in London was on the table for weeks but I hadn't made a decision until after that night."

With a furrowed brow, he shook his head. *Aminah knew about London all along and didn't tell me.* Nic did not voice his inner musings because he was certain he'd unintentionally, yet viciously spew the words at her.

"But when I saw you at Symphony and Tyus's wedding.... when we danced and laughed like nothing changed between us, I knew if I told you about London, our night would've been spent trying to answer why. I just wanted a night to..."

Aminah huffed. Her bottom lip quivered in fear to unleash the words trapped in her mouth.

"You wanted to what?" Nic queried.

Her weary eyes looked directly into his angst ones.

Unwavering, Aminah muttered, "To make love to you, Nic. I just wanted one night to love you."

Nic listened intently as he ogled her. Tear-stained cheeks and puffy eyes only accentuated the intricate features that made her alluring. Even in her despair, her beauty was a symphony of contradictions.

He desperately wanted to kiss her tenderly and brush away her worries and fear. That had been his role for the duration of their relationship. But now, those actions would be a lie. Nic could acknowledge that Aminah silently battled with internal struggles, but so did he. He could not be her solace, not this time.

Nic's well had run dry. His reserves of compassion and adoration were depleted. How could he pour from an empty cup? Aminah pleaded her case but he could not remove his glare from her t-shirt. At least two sizes too big, the white Monroe University School of Art shirt was speckled with variant paint colors. *Malakai,* he thought.

Still holding the bottle of wine in one hand, Nic stretched his arm towards her, tugging at the seam of her T-shirt. Aminah followed the trail from his fingers up his corded arms to his knowing eyes.

Nic grunted through a snicker as he lowered his head.

"You've never really talked about Malakai. About your relationship with him. How it ended. But I'm finally realizing that it *hasn't* ended for you. Although he's gone, you're still connected," Nic uttered, finally lifting his eyes to look at her.

Aminah nibbled her bottom lip nervously, fondling the seam his fingers touched.

"I can't win. I *won't* compete with a ghost. You're still connected... grieving for him."

Although tears saturated her face, Aminah's features remained stoic as she internally wrestled with the complexities of her heart and mind. There was no use debating his assessment. He was right, she'd wept countless tears that carried the memory of love lost. But what Nic didn't know was that while she was burdened with the weight of goodbye, she yearned the lightness of his tender embrace and found solace of what could be.

"And I knew - *I knew* that was your story but I believed that the way I wanted to love you would erase all of that hurt. Love you so good that it lessened your grief."

"And you have, Nic. You did... *you do*."

He shook his head.

"Nah... if that was true, we wouldn't be here, Lov - Aminah," he said, quickly correcting his potential slip of the enduring nickname.

Aminah carefully closed the minimal space separating them. Slowly lifting her hand, she tickled four fingers down his forearm. She braced for his recoil but he did not flinch. Her movements were slow and deliberate; as expected, his touch was cold and tentative.

While she missed the Nicolas who embraced her unapologetically anytime and anyplace, she was responsible for this new version, cautious and apprehensive. But to her surprise, the magnetism and longing they shared did not dissipate.

Still holding the bottle in one hand, Nic palmed her nape with the other, drawing her nearer. Temple to temple, their eyes locked in a silent dance of misunderstanding, secrets, and sorrow. As his alcohol-tinged exhales became her inhales, their breaths mingled in familiarity.

"Nic... You've been drinking. Let's sit down and talk about this."

Closing his eyes, he lightly chuckled before whispering against her lips.

"Yeah... I am drunk. I *been* drunk for you, Aminah. I just need to be numb for a minute," his voice faltered.

"I slept for weeks after you left because the only place I could find you... Hear your voice was my dream." Nic closed his eyes so tight as if he was trying to find moments of happiness with her again.

"This shit hurts," he croaked and Aminah's heart broke.

Her cry was anguished, mirroring the sound of glass shattering into a million pieces. Aminah wasn't sure if an inevitable goodbye was looming, but she grasped him tighter just in case it was on the horizon. With every squeeze she expelled a raw, pained sob, laced with incomprehensible, *"I'm sorry."*

"I gotta go," Nic murmured.

"Nic... please."

Aminah wasn't too proud to beg because she knew she'd fucked up. She clinged to the hem of his shirt as he released himself from her firm clutch. Nic reluctantly stepped away but not before thumping away the fountain of tears running down her swollen cheeks.

"I gotta go, Love," he whispered.

Aminah nodded this time, understanding the need for space. She'd had four months to process what he meant to her. The least she could do was give him the same. Aminah backed away and leaned against the door.

With a final shared glance, they mutely communicated more than words ever could in the moment. Nic flicked his nose, vainly attempting to extinguish the torrent of emotions plaguing him. Seeing her after all this time and on bad terms had him reeling. Nic was certain he would hear her out at some point, but not now. A sudden urge to flee the scene immediately came over him.

Bending over, he placed the wine bottle near her feet and drifted down the hallway, vanishing from visibility.

Aminah slowly bent over to pick up the bottle. She glanced at the beauty of the glass, noticing the intricately carved fireflies. Rubbing her eyes to clear the flood of tears, she scanned the sketched image and immediate recognition dressed her face: a woman, shoeless in a flowy dress, hair bundled in a bun, dancing in a sea of fireflies.

"It's me," she croaked, in awe of the realism.

"Lovie's Dream," she mouthed the words swirling across the bottle.

Then came the uncontrollable soul-stirring sobs.

9

Aminah pulled her black BMW Coupe into a parking space in the back of the building that housed the office of Dr. Jaclyn Bernard Valdez. After the girls' night slash unpacking party with Symphony and Syncere last week, they handed her a large gift bag filled with housewarming gifts. Attached to the bag was a congratulations card from her friends. When they encouraged her to open it, she had no dream that her gift would include an open appointment with the infamous Dr. Jacky.

Both Syncere and Symphony raved about their experience with the Dr. Valdez, whom they lovingly named, the good doctor. Her friends had navigated their own trauma in different ways, but Dr. Valdez was at the root of their healing.

Slowly crawling out of her car, Aminah's nerves pulsed rapidly at even the thought of disclosing her truth. She jerked from the vibration of her phone in her hand. It was a video call from Syncere and Symphony.

"He - hello," Aminah stuttered.

"Hey, Minah. We're just checking on you before your appointment," Syncere's soothing voice chimed.

"This is a fucked up housewarming gift, friends," Aminah fussed, giggling faintly.

"But a necessary one, friend," Syncere retorted.

"Dr. Jacky is going to piss you off so just get ready. I called myself being a smart ass and just sat there quietly at my first few appointments until *the good doctor* reminded me that she still gets paid whether I talk or not," Symphony said, releasing a roaring laugh.

"I was like… *Bitch,* you right. After that, my broken ass couldn't shut up. Dr. Jacky is a bad bitch," she continued.

Symphony's crazy humor was just what Aminah needed.

"Prima, shut up. We agreed that we were calling to help Minah calm down," Syncere uttered, rolling her eyes.

"Minah knows how I get down," Symphony shrugged.

"Mimi, I'm going to share a little wisdom that my then fine ass boyfriend, now sexy ass husband shared with me," Syncere said, blushing.

"Speak from your heart *and* your hurt, Aminah. It's been four years. It's time to clear your conscience… And tell the truth, babe. Ok?"

Aminah nodded.

"We love you, Mi," Symphony sang.

"I love y'all too."

Entering Dr. Jacky's office, Aminah circled her eyes around the light yellow painted waiting room. It looked more like a spa than a therapist's office. She snickered faintly thinking about Symphony's description of the waterfall feature covering half of the wall.

That thing makes me have to pee every time I go in there. Aminah recalled her silly friend's comment.

"Good afternoon," the receptionist squeaked. "Aminah Loveless, correct?"

Aminah nodded.

"Yes. Um, I have a two o'clock appointment. I - I'm a little early," Aminah nervously announced. She'd heeded her friends' warning about being late for a session.

"I'm supposed to give you my phone, right?" she asked.

Aminah was a nervous wreck. Syncere and Symphony had her so anxious about Dr. Jacky's *policies* that she was stumbling over her words.

The receptionist giggled.

"Not just yet, Ms. Loveless. Scan this code to complete the required paperwork. Once you're done, power off your phone and I'll hold it at my desk."

"Thank you."

The release forms and insurance documents took Aminah about ten minutes to complete. Signaling to the receptionist that she was done, she returned to the plush chair to wait for the doctor to finish her lunch.

Aminah blankly stared at the water rolling over the rocks of the waterfall. The gentle sound was meant to be a soothing melody. But her thoughts were a whirlwind of chaos, colliding like a storm instead of the calming trickle of water.

What are you going to tell her, Aminah? The truth? Everything? She mutedly negotiated.

Two dings chimed from her phone. Unlocking the screen, she read the text message and smiled.

Ma: Hey sweetheart. Speaking your truth is cleansing. Do this for you, Aminah Rae. It's time, baby girl. We love you.

Aminah: Thank you, Ma. I love you too.

A mother's intuition and love, she thought.

"Ms. Aminah. Are you ready, my dear?"

Aminah's eyes quickly shot up to connect with a tall, lean figure rocking the hell out of a sleek, short haircut. Black square-shaped frames concealed her hazel eyes, and the sweet smile on her face was a small dose of calm to Aminah's spirit.

"Yes. Yes, I'm ready."

Closing the short distance, Aminah was ready to step into the *unapologetic black girl magic* sanctum that her friends described but Dr. Jacky did not move. Her eyes slowly rolled down to Aminah's feet, staring at her shoes.

"Oh, shit. I mean, shoot," Aminah blurted, quickly removing her sneakers.

Dr. Jacky smirked, stepping aside to allow Aminah to enter her office. Syncere and Symphony were right; the office was beautiful and inviting. A pictorial road map of the doctor's extensive travels decorated the walls, while the framed degrees highlighted her many accomplishments.

"Have a seat wherever you are comfortable," Dr. Jacky said, swaying a finger between the blush-colored couch and lounge chairs.

Aminah opted for the couch. She perched in the middle and criss-crossed her legs then abruptly uncrossed them, placing her feet back on the ground.

"It's fine, Aminah. Get comfortable," Dr. Jacky said, encouraging her.

Silence hung uncomfortably above them like a storm cloud ready to pour. Aminah fidgeted with her fingers while darting her eyes across the room. She looked everywhere but in the doctor's direction.

"I'm sensing that you're a little nervous, my dear. Why?"

Aminah shrugged, blinking away a mountain of tears. A flood of emotions suddenly overcame her. A fight between telling a tale or the truth struggled inside of her.

"I thought you only worked with people who've had traumatic experiences?" Aminah blurted.

"How do you define... traumatic experiences?"

"I don't know... Like rape or abuse. None of those things have happened to me."

"Ok. How do you define abuse, dear?"

Aminah sighed, shaking her head. She was only fifteen minutes into her session and the frustration creasing her face was apparent.

"Abuse... Like physical. You know... if a man puts his hands on a woman," she spewed irritably.

"So abuse is only physical?"

Aminah nodded.

"Yeah. I guess."

Dr. Jacky pursed her lips and nodded.

"Do you believe that there could be other forms of abuse?"

"Like what?" Aminah's forehead creased.

"Verbal mistreatment. Aggressive behaviors. Mental manipulation." Dr. Jacky listed a few.

Aminah flinched at the last description.

"Using your definition... Has a man put his hands on you in an inappropriate way, Aminah?"

Aminah shook her head.

"No."

"Has a man been aggressive with you?"

"No. I don't think so," Aminah stammered her words.

"Has a man been verbally disrespectful?"

Aminah paused, bouncing her eyes around in contemplation.

"I don't think so," she whispered. "Not on purpose, anyway."

"Have you felt mentally manipulated by a man?"

The blank glare Aminah gave Dr. Jacky burned with fury and fear. The uncomfortable silence was one-sided because the good doctor was unmoved.

"Hmm," Dr. Jacky sang with pursed lips then a smile.

There she goes with that damn humming again. What the hell does that mean? Malakai didn't mean the things he would say. He couldn't help it. Aminah mused.

"Are you willing to name the *man* in our *potential* scenarios?" Dr. Jacky probed.

Aminah shook her head.

"There's no one to name," Aminah whimpered, her voice breaking with every syllable.

"OK. Then tell me about Malakai," the doctor said, referring to her iPad, on which she kept patient notes.

Aminah completely forgot about mentioning him in the pre-work journaling Dr. Jacky required.

"What do you want to know?" Aminah questioned, only to give herself an extra minute to determine what she wanted to disclose about Malakai... *If anything*.

"What's your favorite memory of him?"

Memory... There are so many... good and bad. But instantly, a recollection produced a wide smile. Aminah talked non-stop about him: his artistic talent, how smart and funny he was. It felt really good to be reminded of the good times.

"Malakai sounds like an amazing man," Dr. Jacky said, slightly lifting a cheek.

Aminah nodded, licking away the salty tear.

"So, if those are your memories, when did the nightmares begin?"

Aminah shrugged.

"Are they about Malakai?" the doctor interrogated.

Hesitantly, she nodded.

"He never hit me, though. Malakai wouldn't do that," Aminah declared hurriedly, thumbing the scar on her chin.

Dr. Jacky raised a curious brow.

"I never said that he did, my dear."

They stared at each other for a long minute but no words were exchanged.

"May I read you something?" Dr. Jacky asked.

Aminah nodded, then uttered, "Sure."

I used to dream about Malakai, but now, they are the most terrifying nightmares. I wake up in a cold sweat, my heart pounding like it's going to burst out of my chest. It's always dark and the air feels heavy, almost suffocating. But I'm never in our house. Sometimes I'm outside or at school. I can hear his footsteps in my sleep. At first, I feel excited when he appears in the doorway, but he's different. His eyes are cold, almost lifeless, and his sinister smile makes my blood run cold. When I call his name so maybe he could snap out of the trance, he starts chasing me. I run so fast. It's dark and foggy but I just keep running. Finally, I make it to the garage and get in his car. Just as I'm about to drive away, he bangs on the window and I wake up.

"This journal entry is dated September of twenty-twenty one. Was this your first nightmare?"

Aminah bobbed her head again.

"Yes," she cried, swiping both cheeks.

"I don't want to talk about this. Malakai did not abuse me," Aminah bellowed.

Dr. Jacky nodded her head, whispering, "Ok. Ok."

The good doctor was an expert at the unwavering stare. Her poker face was priceless.

"Would you like to talk about Nic?"

Aminah lifted her eyes, a glimmer of sunshine kindled in her eyes.

"No. Not right now."

Dr. Jacky slowly nodded.

"Aminah, let me offer you this," she said. Placing her iPad on the table, she leaned forward and searched Aminah's face until their eyes collided.

"My dear, abuse can come in many forms. Yes, physical abuse is easily recognizable because in most cases, the victim is left with visible scars. On the other hand, *emotional* abuse is what we therapists like to call the invisible trauma. Increased anxiety, chronic depression, amongst other psychological problems, brought on by the actions of another."

"Hmm," Aminah hummed snarkily, but a silent storm of emotions quaked in the depths of her eyes.

"So you see, Ms. Aminah, verbal maltreatment and emotional abuse can be the hardest forms to detect. We often label them misunderstandings or make excuses like the person was having a bad day, because they don't necessarily leave an obvious blemish to the naked eye. But *I* see *you*, my dear."

A lone tear raced down Aminah's face as fast as her need to escape. Rage, confusion, and heartache thunderously crashed, leaving her feeling battered and exposed.

Aminah croaked, licking away the salty dampness from the corner of her mouth.

"What do you see?"

Dr. Jacky removed her glasses and leaned in further with her hands clasped.

"I see a beautiful young woman who is afraid to define whatever it is she's been through as a… traumatic experience," Dr. Jacky surmised, referring back to Aminah earlier comment.

Aminah audibly huffed,

"Why would I be afraid of that?"

"Because then you would have to admit that you, my dear, are a victim," Dr. Jacky relayed, removing her glasses and placing them on the table.

"And admittance is the hardest part of healing. So, whenever you are ready to free yourself of all of this baggage…" her voice fizzled momentarily as her finger swirled, gesturing towards Aminah.

"My door is always open."

10

"See ya later, Justin," Aminah said, pushing the door open to leave Davenport Realty.

"I'll see you tomorrow, Justin. Remember I'll be out in the morning for the field trip with the twins," Syncere announced to her boss, as she followed behind Aminah.

"He gets finer and finer every time I see him," Aminah bantered.

"You know Justin is like a brother to me so I don't see it."

"Chile, Stevie Wonder can see that shit."

"Now you know damn well Stevie can see," Syncere joked.

The duo spurted a loud cackle as they walked toward Syncere's car.

"When is girls' night at your place?" Syncere asked.

"Anytime," Aminah returned. "I still have a few boxes to unpack and some painting to do so you ladies can come over any time."

Aminah was going to the Brown Bean when she ran into Syncere. Her condo was right above the realty office so she and her friend had seen a lot of each other lately.

"Ok. Well, let me get out of her before the twins -"

Syncere abruptly paused the rest of her sentence when she noticed the bewildered look on Aminah's face. Syncere turned her head toward her friend's gaze and their eyes landed on Nic... and Fallon. Laughing quite comfortably, the pair walked towards a white Lexus truck parked in front of Nic's bar. He opened her door and she extended her arms to hug him.

Aminah quickly turned away to prevent seeing the gut-wrenching act that she was certain would follow the hug. She took a deep breath, but the slightly erratic rise and fall of her chest couldn't be controlled.

She hadn't had direct contact with Nic since he showed up on her doorstep a little over a week ago. They lived less than a block away from each other so it was inevitable that they frequented the same places on Main Street. The day she saw him in the coffee shop, she quickly dipped into the beauty salon next door before she was seen.

Aminah's eyes lifted to Syncere seeking a comrade in this situation. But for the first time in... *forever*, her friend's eyes did not spark with its usual compassion-filled sympathy.

Syncere huffed as she rubbed her growing belly.

"I am going to do my best to channel my dear cousin and your dear friend for a moment," she said teasingly, referring to Symphony.

Placing a firm hand on Aminah's shoulder, Syncere muttered, "You're fucking up, friend. Get your shit together or watch another woman love on your man."

Planting a kiss against Aminah's blushed cheek, Syncere returned to her normal sweet disposition and ordered, "Go talk to him, Minah... *now*."

Aminah did not move while she watched Syncere drive away. With tightly sealed eyes, she refused to turn around. She swallowed hard to clear away impending emotions. Taking a deep breath, Aminah turned around, prepared to face him... but Nic was gone.

A couple of hours later, Nic was in his office at the back of the bar, working on another stack of legal documents. A short chime dinged, indicating that someone was at the front of the building. He glanced at the security monitors and saw a familiar figure pacing before the bar window.

It was Aminah. She quickly trekked back and forth while clutching a box to her chest. He snickered, shaking his head because as mad as he was, Aminah was still the prettiest woman he'd ever encountered. There was a part of him that wanted to ignore her, make her ass stay outside. But the part that couldn't erase her words from his psyche wanted to hear more about her desire for him to love her.

"Are you trespassing on my property? Do I need to call the police?" Nic spoke through the intercom typically reserved for delivery services.

Aminah looked around, searching for the voice until she saw the small speaker next to the door. She shook her head then pushed the button to speak.

"Can we talk?"

Nic intently watched her on the monitor for a long heartbeat. He seriously considered saying no, but he still had so many questions. And honestly, he'd had a chance to think after his drunken tirade and wanted to hear her out.

"Give me a second," he responded.

Sighing heavily, he lifted from the desk chair and slowly walked to the front of the bar. Unlocking the door, he held it open for her to enter. Aminah tiptoed into the space, carefully regarding him as if he would kick her out at any second.

"Hey," she said.

"Hello. What can I do for you, Ms. Loveless?" His tone wasn't cold, but it wasn't welcoming either.

"I saw you come in here earlier and I just... um, I just wanted to see if we can talk."

Nic motioned his hand towards the leather bar stool. Aminah cracked a faint smile before settling in the seat. He was curious about the box she held but didn't pry. Rounding the bar, Nic stood on the opposite side of her.

"Do you want a drink?" he asked, preparing a beverage for himself.

"Is Lovie's Dream available?"

Nic paused mid-pour, peering up from his glass.

"You tried it?"

She shook her head.

"No. I wanted to have it with you."

He stared at her. Shit, practically through her, he was so angry. Aminah had the nerve to walk into his establishment with those pretty ass eyes and pouty ass lips, dressed down just the way he liked her in those damn fitted joggers, cropped t-shirt, and sneakers.

He shook his head.

"Nah. Lovie's Dream is not ready," Nic uttered, his words having a deeper meaning that she comprehended.

Aminah pursed her lips while nodding.

"Water is fine then," she whispered.

Nic poured the bottled sparkling water over a few ice cubes and added a lemon and lime, just as she liked it.

Sliding it across the bar top, he said, "I've said all I have to say, so talk."

"I brought you something," Aminah said, lifting the box she had secured to her chest.

It appeared heavier than it seemed when she placed it on the bar. Nic glanced at her, the box, and then back up at her. He was suspicious of her motives and a little confused. *She'd left for four months without a text message response, but she's bringing gifts as if that will fix things between us.*

Nic didn't try to erase the scowl staining his face as he lifted the lid. Pulling back the tissue paper, his narrowed eyes softened. He gazed at her but made no effort to speak.

"London was an opportunity for me to figure out my next move. It was a short term assignment with long-term potential. The day the committee offered me the permanent role, I asked for some time to consider it. When I left the office, I decided to walk back to my apartment and stumbled into this quaint wine bar that I'd never noticed before. The sign in the window read, 'Grapes and Mash'."

Aminah looked at Nic for the first time since she started talking. He was stoic but listening.

"I practically stormed into the place because I was shocked to see the name," she pointed toward the Grapes and Mash logo on the window of Nic's bar.

"The bar had a vintage feel and held so much history. And this plaque," she motioned to the opened box. "It immediately caught my attention and I immediately thought about this place... *you.*"

A light mist dusted her eyes as she gazed at him.

"I asked the bartender where I could find the plaque like this and he said it was one of a kind. He was an asshole though," Aminah snickered.

"He didn't believe that I knew what the words meant. He was like, '*Oh sweetheart, you have no clue what that means, cutie pie.*'" She rolled her eyes, mocking the man's voice.

Nic tried his damndest to stop his chuckle, but he laughed at her horrible attempt at an accent. The faint smile forming on his face made her giggle.

"So I made a bet with him. If I could explain the process, he would take it off the wall and give it to me. If I couldn't, I had to agree to a date with him."

His previous lighthearted guise quickly held that scowl again. That *date* comment made him wonder if Aminah dated anyone while in London. *Did she fuck somebody?*

Just the thought of it made him pour another drink. *This girl is going to turn me into an alcoholic.*

"As you can see, I won," she laughed.

"Please open it, Nic," she requested.

He pulled back the last piece of paper covering the item. The rolling plain of a vineyard was carved into the walnut-colored wooden base. Raised metal lettering was beautifully written in bold, shiny script. It was a beautiful piece of artwork and was perfect for his space.

Nic's eyes danced between his gift and *his gift*... Aminah. For the past four months, he was convinced that he was never on her mind but it was clear that she'd thought of him.

"This was a sign," she said.

"A sign of what?"

"A sign that I needed to come home. I declined the job and hopped on a plane -"

"What do you want, Lov -" Nic blurted, then cleared his throat.

"Aminah, what do you want from me?"

"I don't have any expectations or want anything other than for you to know I am so sorry. I was wrong. Nic, I - "

"You've said that already. But what exactly are you sorry for? Leaving? No wait, maybe fucking me then burning out. Or maybe you're sorry for not answering my calls. The list could go on but what exactly are you sorry for, Aminah?" Nic cocked his head, brow furrowed as he glared at her, waiting for a response.

"All of it, Nic," Aminah shouted, standing from the bar stool, hands flailing.

"I'm sorry for everything. I miss you, Nic. I miss my friend. I lov -" Aminah's words faltered.

Resting her elbows on the bar, she lowered her head into her hands.

"I just want my friend back," Aminah whimpered.

Nic surveyed her, but he remained wordless. Sincerity and a plea for forgiveness saddened her pretty eyes. He believed that his love battled a host of demons, but Nic was exhausted; he couldn't fight for her anymore. Aminah had to fight for herself.

"I thought you said you didn't want anything from me," Nic spat indignantly.

His voice was laced with all of the venom Aminah knew she deserved. But the shit still hurt. She chewed the inside of her jaw, vainly attempting to quell her tears. Aminah nodded while tapping her nails against the bar nervously. Instinctively, she wrapped her hand around Nic's and pulled his hand to her lips, resting three soft kisses to the top of his hand.

He stilled, swallowing hard in response to her gesture. Three kisses to her temple, cheeks, hands, wherever, was usually Nic's routine. It was his silent way of saying, *I Love You,* but what message was Aminah sending.

Is she trying to tell me she loves me? Nic mused. He recalled the night they blessed each other with orgasm after orgasm.

They were spent, but sleep wouldn't come for him. Nic intently watched Aminah. The beauty in the rise and fall of her chest. The delightful buzz of her snoring. He wanted to bottle the magic of her beauty and carry it wherever he went. Smiling, Nic stroked his fingertip down the arc of her face. She squirmed and shifted to her side but didn't wake. Positioning himself directly behind her, he rested his chin on the cloud of curls sprawled across the pillow. She nuzzled into his broad frame.

"I'm so sorry. I want him. I think I love this man." Aminah's mumble was muffled but comprehendible.

Nic's eyes widened, and he was awestricken yet comforted by her words. Kissing her temple one more time, he fell into a deep slumber.

Aminah's disconnection from his hand caused him to return to the present moment. Nic always wondered why she was apologizing in her sleep, but her departure was his answer. She knew that she was leaving. She knew that she would hurt him. And that was what vexed Nic the most.

He watched as she hurriedly rushed towards the door. Nic sighed, massaging his nape in exasperation. Nic's head was reminded of the fondness he carried for this woman, urging him to go after her. But his heart... his heart carried memories, too—recollections of the night they made love, the moment his dream turned into an ugly nightmare.

Fuck!

Nic shot across the room. The delicate touch on her elbow was barely detectable, like a whisper against her skin. But it arrested her, nonetheless, halting her escape. Aminah desperately wanted to breathe, but exhaling would sever the spell of intimacy that enveloped them.

Nic slid a hand down her forearm and clasped her hand in his. With a wordless gesture, he cradled his other arm around her waist. Hesitantly, yet firmly, he drew her body in closer and tighter until any space was nonexistent.

Quiet loomed for an extending heartbeat. The flustered sigh they harmoniously released played like a melody in the silence, a wretched reminder of the pain they carried and the depth of their bond. Nicolas leaned in, nudging his nose against her ear. A wave of electricity coursed through her veins, sending goosebumps racing across her flesh. He swiped his thumb across the pond of desire rippling across her skin.

"I missed you, Love."

She lowered her eyes, a glint of relief graced her face. Cheek to cheek, Aminah felt his smooth skin against hers, swiping side-to-side as he shook his head.

"But friends have to trust each other. I… I don't trust you, Aminah. I can't." He informed her, in a tone just above a whisper.

Aminah sharply inhaled, her breath hitched in her throat. As Nic's words sank in, disbelief colored her features. She knew that her return would not be easy, however, Aminah had no dream that rekindling a friendship with Nic would be an impossible scenario.

"I can't keep fixing things I didn't break."

Disbelief rendered her speechless. Muted tears streaked her cheeks. She swiped them away aggressively before lifting her eyes to search his eyes for a sign of… *something.* Aminah was thankful to see familiarity, adoration…, and love dancing in his eyes. But the angst and mistrust could not be ignored in his vacant stare.

Aminah rose to her tip-toes and kissed his cheek.

Nodding, she whispered, “I understand. Take care, okay.”

She languidly slipped from his hold. He stared at her with each step towards the door until Aminah was about to break the gaze.

“Lovie,” Nic said.

Aminah paused her pursuit and lifted a brow.

“I accept your apology.”

11

Aminah spent the beautiful Friday morning with her new team. She'd been in her new role for a month and loved every minute. While she missed engaging with students, she was ecstatic about the opportunity to make the Monroe University Art Foundation a community staple. Adhering to her schedule with her previous staff, half-day Fridays, Aminah closed the office at noon.

She practically ran into the Brown Bean because the iced caramel macchiato had been calling Aminah's name all morning. Waving at a few familiar faces, she stood in the growing line and patiently waited to place her order.

"Order for Nic," the barista belted out.

Aminah's head was immediately on a swivel in search of *him.*

Girl, it's a million men named Nic. Calm down.

Since leaving his bar almost two months ago, she'd tried her best to stay clear of Nicolas Touissant. His message was clear; he did not trust her. No trust, no friendship, *no nothing.*

But it seemed that a devilish power had another idea.

Aminah could not hide. When she'd arrive at the gym, he would be leaving. Most mornings she would see him walking from the coffee shop just as she was about to enter. It was bad enough that they shared mutual friends, so those activities had been awkward enough. They exchange a dull, "*hi*" or "*how are you,*" but nothing of substance.

"That's me," his baritone boomed from across the room, sending chills down her middle.

Aminah licked her lips and hadn't even tasted her coffee's rich, nutty flavors yet. Shit, Nic looked good enough to sip, lick, and devour. Dressed in a cocoa brown slacks and crisp white shirt that hugged his muscular form in all of the right places. Grabbing his order, he smiled and nodded in appreciation, exuding an air of sophistication and charm that left her breathless.

Aminah was so winded by his presence, haphazardly croaked, "Hey there," an octave louder than necessary.

Nic glanced up from his phone. To her surprise, a little of the smile he shared with the barista was leftover for her.

"Hey. How are you?" he said, standing beside her in line.

"Good. Good. How are you?"

Nic nodded, then uttered, "Pretty good."

With each glance, each breath they took, silence hung between them like a dense fog clouding their minds as they struggled to find the right words to break the tension.

"I can help who's next," the cashier announced.

"Well, let me not keep her waiting. It was good seeing you, Nic."

"I was going to find a seat if... If you'd like to join me."

Aminah almost tripped over her feet as she placed her order.

"Um, yeah. Yes, I'd like that. I'll find you in a sec."

Nic nodded then turned, circling his eyes throughout the crowded shop to find a space. Aminah grabbed her coffee and took several deep breaths before finding him seated at a small table near the window facing Main Street.

"This seat taken?" she teased.

Snickering, Nic stood to pull out her chair.

"Nah. It's reserved just for you."

Aminah blushed and got comfortable in her seat, but she didn't miss the effervescent lightness of his words or his mood.

"So how's the new gig?" he asked.

"So far, so good. My office is beautiful and has a great view of Forest Park," Aminah responded giddily.

"Seems like you're happy with your decision."

She nodded, sipping her coffee.

"I am. I have a great team that will be growing. And I still get to do what I love. Just not in the classroom," she paused momentarily. "But I can't lie. I do miss tapping into those brilliant and innovative young minds."

"I'm sure you can find other ways to do that. There's plenty of schools right here in the city that need a teacher like you. Even if it's just to volunteer your time."

Aminah faintly smiled.

"Yeah. You're right. That's actually not a bad idea."

"I've never been short of those. You ever need to brainstorm ideas... I'm your man."

They both sipped their drinks to mute any reaction to the innuendo. Their bubbly stares were laced with a hint of caution and desire. What they privately thought would be a tense moment was actually a breath of fresh air.

With every passing minute, Nic and Aminah did not miss a beat. With every joke and playful nudge, it was like old times between friends. Their conversation became a musical of laughter.

"Aminah, this was great but I have to go," Nic said, silencing an incoming message on his phone.

"Of course. Of course. Me too. I'm meeting Symphony, Syncere, and the kids at the park."

Nic stood and so did she. He extended his hand for her to walk ahead of him.

Don't stare at her ass. Don't stare at her ass. He challenged silently but failed miserably.

Aminah was simply dressed in a fitted skirt, tank top, and denim jacket but there was nothing simple about her ass. It was perfectly plump and Nic desperately wanted to cradle it in his hands one more time.

"Thanks again. This was fun," Aminah said once they walked outside.

Nic nodded.

"Nicky. Nic," a woman's voice trilled from the direction of his bar.

"Nomi. What's up? I was just about to call you."

Naomi took quick steps towards them as if she was on a mission. Aminah's smile faded in response to the displeased guise his sister wore.

"What are you doing with her?" Naomi barked.

She darted an evil glare towards Aminah, dragging her eyes from the diminishing grin on her face to the hand she had on Nic's arm.

"Naomi. Stop," Nic grumbled.

He knew all too well how protective his little sister was of him and where this exchange could go. Naomi was his listening ear when Aminah left so she knew *everything*.

"Stop?" she yelled questioningly. "Please don't tell me you believed whatever lame apology she gave for leaving like that." Naomi spoke as if Aminah wasn't standing there.

"Nomi. I got this. So stop."

Naomi was about to speak when Aminah chimed in.

"No, Nic. She has a right to be upset," she said before focusing on his sister, raising a brow giving permission for Naomi to continue.

"You are all he *ever* talks about. His *friend* Aminah. But I know my brother and I know when he wants something, he's relentless in his pursuit. If he didn't love you as a friend *and more*, he damn sure would not allow himself to be strung along. But then you have the nerve to leave. I don't know what kinda friends you have, but *real friends* don't do that shit," Naomi spat.

Aminah nodded.

"You're right. I was wrong, Naomi. Dead ass wrong. And a shitty friend. You and Nic have every right not to trust me. Shit, to hate me."

"I don't hate you, Lovie," Nic interrupted, dismantling her thoughts immediately.

"I've apologized to your brother. He accepted my apology and also made his stance very clear. This was merely a run in between old friends. No more no less," Aminah looked at Naomi and then focused her attention on the only person that mattered at the moment.

"It was good seeing you. I'll see you around," she uttered, flashing a subtle closed mouth smile.

Nic nodded, eyeing Aminah until she disappeared down the street.

"Nicky... Don't," Naomi demanded.

"I'm a big boy, Nomi. I got this."

Nic continued to stare down the street until the last glimpse of Aminah was out of sight. Did he have this? *What the fuck am I doing?*

He kissed her forehead, ignoring his sister's uneasy stare. Draping his arm over her shoulders, they started towards his bar.

"Now, what's so urgent that you are blowing up my phone."

Nic quickly realized why his sister was texting him nonstop. She was preparing the food for the bar's soft opening later that night, and everything that could go wrong did. The brand new wine chiller was on the brink, and one of the bourbon taps was not working. Naomi was on a rampage because the avocado for her sauce was not to her liking.

After resolving the problems, Nic schlepped up the steps to his apartment. He needed some time to clear his head before he'd be meeting and greeting guests. Tonight was an invitation only event to generate some buzz in the community and celebrate with his family and friends. *Friends... Aminah.*

Nic undressed and showered in record time. Wrapped in nothing but a towel, he laid back on the bed holding his phone above his face. His finger hovered over Aminah's contact because she was the only *friend* he had not invited. Today was the first day since she'd been back that they actually held a conversation beyond two to three words.

As much as he hated to admit it, it felt good being in her presence. Being able to laugh and talk to her like they used to. Aminah seemed different... lighter. She illuminated a glow and confidence that was intriguing. *Who was this new woman?*

Nic was about to mention the event until he saw his sister

storm towards them. Amid the chaos, he forgot to discuss it with her. But Aminah was the first person he told about Grapes and Mash, so he wanted her to be there.

Fuck it.

Nic: Hey again. It was good seeing…

He shook his head, deleting part of the text message.

Nic: Hey again. I forgot to mention that I'm having an event at the bar tonight. Just a few clients and business owners on Main. The crew will be there too so feel free to stop by. [peace sign emoji]

Aminah had been in the park with her friends and godchildren all afternoon. After ice cream, they all went to Syncere's house, where the kids were bathed and fast asleep. While Aminah and Symphony enjoyed glasses of wine, the mommy-to-be indulged in sparkling water.

"Sooo… I ran into Nic today."

"We've been together for hours and you're just spilling this tea," Symphony fussed.

"It wasn't that big of a deal. We were both at the Brown Bean and he invited me to join him."

Her friends were hanging on every word, thirsty for more.

"And?" Syncere stated, asking for more details.

"And we just talked," she smirked

"And it felt really good. Too good," Aminah muttered, plopping down on the couch.

"Until his little big sister came stomping in my face like she was Sophia marching towards Celie," she chuckled and her friends joined in.

"You fucked with my brother," Symphony said, mimicking the infamous scene in the *Color Purple*.

"Girl, Naomi don't play about Nic," Syncere howled.

"Tell me about it," Aminah giggled.

Aminah took another sip of wine with her feet propped up on the ottoman when her phone chimed, indicating a text message. Those pretty brown eyes widened in surprise when she saw the sender.

"Nic texted me," she yelped, dropping her phone on the couch as if it was on fire.

"Ok... What did he say?" Symphony asked.

"I don't know. I didn't read the message."

"Well, read it, silly girl," Syncere bantered.

Aminah swiped the screen to unlock her phone. Her big grin shined brighter and brighter with every word she read.

"Why didn't y'all tell me he was having an event at the bar tonight?"

Syncere pursed her lips; those gray eyes danced around skittishly.

"Because you weren't invited," Symphony declared unapologetically. "As a matter of fact, we need to get ready. Prima, what time is the babysitter getting here?"

Aminah rolled her eyes.

"Well I guess the three of us need to get ready because I'm going," Aminah announced, shoving her phone in Symphony's direction.

Syncere peeked over her cousin's shoulder to read the message.

Squealing, she said, "I know that's right, Minah. You betta go get your man, girl."

"You know Fallon will be there, right?" Symphony inquired.

Aminah nodded, keenly smirking.

"Ok then, bitch. Let the games begin," Symphony squealed.

. . .

An hour later, the trio was dressed and ready to party. They kissed their babies goodbye and headed outside to the truck where King and Tyus were waiting. King looked at his wife warily in the high heels he despised. Syncere almost died giving birth to the twins, and he was not taking any chances this time.

"Princess," he growled.

"I have flats in my purse, babe. Once we get a few pictures, these are coming off," she said, kissing him to quiet his fussing.

King shook his head.

"Hard headed," Symphony whispered.

"Really, sweet pea? You were in heels the day you went into labor so you can't talk," Tyus exclaimed, kissing his wife before helping her into the truck.

Aminah laughed as she digested the love and happiness wafting in the air. These moments were a bittersweet concoction of admiration and yearning. Her longing for a life partner to be cherished and adored resided in one of her best friends. He was just a fifteen-minute ride away, but Aminah was uncertain if their shared profound connection could be rekindled.

The crew walked into Grapes and Mash about thirty minutes after the start time and the place was already packed. Trays of hors d'oeuvres prepared by Naomi floated through the room while smooth R&B resounded through the speakers.

Aminah felt the familiar tingling sensation trekking down her spine in his presence. He was across the room schmoozing and being great as usual. Nic was like a quiet storm; he moved with the grace and poise of a king.

She just wanted to stare at him undetected for as long as possible. He was beautiful. All of his magnetism, charm, and sexiness had her twisting and squirming. The tight faux leather leggings pressing against her pulsating clit was not a good idea.

Aminah snagged a glass from the server's tray, gulping down the unknown liquid. She needed to quell the temptation to attack him right in front of these people. Her body had not been touched since Nicolas, not even by her own hands.

Nic spotted her immediately when he felt a flutter in his chest. He despised the sudden surge of excitement but was happy she came. Their interaction earlier was the gentle breeze against his skin he did not know he needed. But the destruction she caused still haunted him. He wanted to trust her, to reignite the tangible force they always shared. But if he was being honest, Nic was afraid.

"Hey. This is a great turn out," Fallon said, animatedly clapping her hands.

"We should celebrate tonight," she whispered, tightening the small gap between them.

Nic wore a bemused expression. He and Fallon had only been intimate once since they became acquainted again. And they both agreed that it was a mistake. Nic and Fallon cared for each other because they had history but moved on and found new loves. Their one night together was a drunken encounter to numb the loss of the ones they truly desired. So Fallon's proposition was surprising.

"Fallon. You know that's not what we're on," Nic reminded her. His tone dripped with sincerity… empathy.

"You don't want me. *We* don't want *this.* We were empty pleasures for each other, desperate to silence the pain we felt from the ones we truly love," he continued, nudging her chin. "Go get your man back, Fallon."

She snickered, smiling as she swiped the corners of her eyes.

"Take your own advice, sir. Go get your girl," Fallon urged, motioning her head across the room where Aminah was talking to her friends.

"She messed up... Big time. But it takes a lot of courage to apologize. To show up, support you, even when the future of your relationship is unclear."

Fallon kissed Nic on the cheek, grabbed her purse from the chair then waved a muted goodbye as she strode towards the exit. He smiled, mutedly wishing her the best as he watched her leave. His eyes quickly navigated to Aminah. Although dressed in all black, she wasn't hard to find.

Nic lifted his glass in greeting and she did the same. He wanted to move but his feet were shackled to the floor. Aminah sensed his hesitation, comprehending that she would need to make a move. Shuffling through the crowd, she approached him with a shy smile brightening her face.

"Hey. Congratulations. This place is wonderful."

"Thank you," Nic sighed. "I'm happy with the final product. Good review on the bourbon so far. The new wines too."

Aminah nodded, circling her finger around her wine glass.

"The wine. Lovie's Dream, it's... perfect."

Nic shrugged.

"I had the *perfect* inspiration," he said, allowing one side of his mouth to resemble a smile.

Nic chatted with prospective buyers and other local business owners throughout the night but kept Aminah close. They hadn't exchanged many words since saying hello, but she was right by his side with every move he made.

He refused to let her slip away despite her few attempts to retreat. His strong arms latched onto anything to keep her near. Aminah gave his hand three squeezes again, silently promising that she would never let him go this time.

Raising on her tiptoes, she whispered in his ear, "I'm going to the ladies room."

He nodded, reluctantly releasing her hand. Nic joined his friends near the bar. Syncere and Symphony sat in the plush chairs, while King and Tyus talked beside them.

"You've been busy, man. You get some good prospects?" King asked, exchanging daps with his friend.

"Hell yeah. The bourbon has been a win, man," Nic chuckled proudly.

"And this wine... *Bay-bee,* it's fire," Symphony sang.

"I can't wait to drop this baby so I can indulge." Syncere pouted. "But thank you for the sparkling cider, Nic," she said, lifting her glass.

"You know I got you, sis."

"Where's Aminah?" Symphony asked.

"Bathroom," Nic responded.

Hopeful grins and inquisitive stares danced between the crew. Everyone wanted to know the verdict but did not dare ask about the obvious alliance or re-alliance between Nic and Aminah. Syncere discreetly nudged Symphony with her foot, encouraging her to do what she does best.... *pry.*

"So, Nic. Are you outta your feelings now? Y'all good?" Symphony spat.

Syncere's eyes bulged in disbelief.

Throwing a ball of tissue at her cousin, Syncere gritted through her teeth, "Prima."

"Babe," Tyus scolded at the same time.

Nic chuckled, finessing the corners of his mouth. He was all too familiar with Symphony's silly, sometimes uncivilized nature.

"I'm taking it one day at a time," he retorted.

"She's really sorry and she needs you, Nic. But you're right, y'all should take it slow," Syncere reasoned.

He nodded, noticing Aminah approaching. Two sets of compassionate gray eyes gazed at her, making it obvious that she was the subject of the conversation.

The friends silently lingered when Syncere uttered, "It's past my bedtime. Bae, are you ready?" she asked, extending her hand for King to help her up.

He nodded.

"That's our ride so we're heading out too," Tyus said, pulling Nic in for a brotherly handshake before he grabbed his wife's hand.

Hugs and see-ya-laters floated between the friends as they approached the door. Aminah followed behind the group when Nic fingered the chain belt on her waist and pulled her back towards him.

"I'm about to wrap this up. I can walk you home if you don't mind waiting," Nic suggested. His lips hovered just inches apart from hers.

An explosion denoted in her center. The wanton tension crackling between them was electric. He stared at her, anticipating a response, but his bourbon-flavored breaths had her spellbound. He lifted a questioning… *Pleading* brow.

A soft, coy smile graced her lips, whispering hushed secrets, inviting him to explore the mysteries locked away in her mind.

"Ok."

12

Aminah sat at the bar enjoying another glass of Lovie's Dream as she watched Nic talk to the last guests. He bid them farewell, locked the door, then turned off the signs in the window. Pausing to collect himself, he slowly turned to face the beauty and the beast who broke his heart.

For weeks Nic contemplated Aminah's apology. But more importantly, he considered how and if he would respond. The rational part of his mind screamed for him to be released from her hold on him, but his heart rebelled every time he collided with her since she returned.

Tonight, Aminah felt like his Lovie. She offered comfort and familiarity that he deeply missed, a lightness that he had not experienced for over one hundred and twenty days.

"My gift looks good up there," he said, nodding toward the wall.

The plaque was prominently placed behind the bar for

everyone to see. She followed his sightline and smiled, hoping it was yet another example of Nic lowering his guard. One step closer to regaining his trust.

"It does. I'm glad it worked out," she said, pausing as they stared at each other.

Nic was still standing near the door while she was at the bar. Their energy was overwhelming. Memories of their lovemaking flickered like stars in the sky as Eric Roberson sang about being picture perfect. For Aminah, they often danced in her mind like fireflies.

"Can I help you clean up around here?" she muttered, attempting to break the uncomfortable silence.

He shook his head but did not move from the distant position.

"Why are you so far away?" she asked, despising the break in her voice.

Rubbing his hand down the valley of waves in his hair, he released an exasperated breath.

"Because if I come any closer, I can't be responsible for what I might do."

"What do you want to do?"

"I want to kiss you, Aminah, but I want to shake the shit out of you too," Nic snickered, shaking his head.

"One minute I want you around, and the next I am reminded —"his voice trailed off, not bothering to rehash what had already been discussed.

"I'm confused, Love," he confessed but unhurriedly began to walk in her direction.

"I understand."

"Do you?" Nic asked, gaining momentum to narrow the space.

In an instant, oxygen refused to supply her lungs when he

opened her legs to step into the gap. The heat of their proximity threatened to engulf them in a whirlwind of longing and need. Rage burned in his eyes, but his tender touch left Aminah torn between the desire to embrace him and the instinct to flee.

With his hand fisted at her waist, it felt like time stood still. Suspended between his imposing arms, their gazes lock as he leaned in. Nic inhaled the citrusy aroma of the wine lingering on her lips. That's how tantalizingly close they were. Harmoniously, their hearts pounded in anticipation. Anticipation of what, they were unsure.

"Nah. I don't think you understand. Aminah, I know your favorite foods. I know that you hate pickles and onions on burgers but love them with fried fish. I know that your right foot is more ticklish than the left. I know that it takes at least thirty two strokes up and down your back before you fall asleep. Lovie, I can even guess when it's your time of the month." Nic rested his forehead against hers.

"But I have no clue who you are, Aminah Rae Loveless."

She cupped his face with trembling hands, tracing the tip of her nose across his lips and cheeks.

"Don't say that. You know me, Nic."

"I know what's on *the surface*, Love. Sometimes I wish I could walk around in your mind. Uncover the secrets that are tucked away behind those beautiful eyes. Find the hurt you have barricaded in the depths of your heart. I want to know what's caused the shattered pieces of uncertainty floating around in that magnificent mind."

Nic thumped away silent teardrops that narrated only excerpts of her complicated story.

He cracked a slight smile and kissed her forehead and nose,

then their lips met in a tender embrace. Nic began to pull back, but Aminah refused to let him go, and he obliged. Her kiss was deep but bore a gentle caress that screamed for forgiveness.

"Mmmm, Aminah," he groaned, fisting her waist with one hand while the other lazily traversed up her body to grasp her nape.

Aminah may have been concerned about the firmness of his grip with any other man, but with Nic, she welcomed his strength... In every form. His reciprocity awakened every nerve ending in her body. Wanton waves of pleasure shot straight to her pussy.

Need dripped from her lips as she traced her tongue down his neck. Grabbing his ass, she pulled him closer, eliminating any room for error. His swollen dick pressed against her oasis. *Grind, knead, press, repeat*, was the preferred cadence.

"Ah, Nic. Please. Please. I'm sorry. I'm sorry," Aminah moaned, as his tongue was now taking a journey down her neck, nestling in her cleavage.

Aminah needed this release. Shit, she craved it. The desire to rip her clothes off, hop on the bar top, and beg him to fuck her was urgent. As if he was reading her mind, Nic palmed two handfuls of ass and scooped her up. Aminah's dream came true. She found herself perched on the bar, legs wide open, and blouse partially unbuttoned.

As their passion ignited, their exchange was frenzied and feverish. Uncoordinated touches and kisses increased the intensity of their maddening foreplay. They were addicts, addicted to the worst kind of drug, leaving them intoxicated with no desire to descend from the delicious high.

"Shit, Love," Nic mumbled, pushing up her bra to reveal her breasts.

Aminah tossed her head back, knocking over a few glasses as he nibbled and licked her nipples.

"Oh my god," she screamed, anticipating what was next when Nic fingered the waistband of her leggings.

Knock. Knock. Knock.

They both audibly gasped in response to the banging against the glass door. *Fuck!* He wasn't sure if he thought or spoke the word. Thank God he'd pulled down the privacy shades so no one could see in.

"Yo, Nic. Your car is still out here if you're in there. They're towing tonight," a bass-filled voice trilled.

Nic quickly helped Aminah get herself together before he trotted to the door. Peeking around the shade, he saw Jericho, an acquaintance and neighborhood cop.

Stepping outside, he said, "What's up, J? Good looking out."

"No problem, man. Tonight was good?" Jericho asked.

Nic nodded.

"Couldn't have been better."

"You got about an hour before they start clearing the street," Jericho warned.

"Thanks again, man."

Nic freed a deep exhale before walking back into his establishment. Closing the door, he leaned against it, staring at her. Aminah was no longer on the bar but Nic could practically smell the need seeping from her pores.

"I, um... I should take you home," he uttered.

Aminah flashed him a faux smile but she nodded in agreement.

"Yeah."

She stood by the door while Nic turned off the rest of the lights and set the alarm. They quietly and slowly strolled the few blocks to her place. Arriving at her door, she scanned the keyfob to enter. Nic held onto the handle, boxing Aminah between his body and the door. Resuming their usual stance, he meshed his head with hers. They floated in care and confusion for a long minute.

"I'm so fucking scared to trust you, but I'm more scared to lose this," he whispered, allowing his lips to brush against her her.

Aminah's eyelids dropped through a breathy exhale.

"Look at me," she requested but he did not obey.

"Nic, please. Look at me," she cupped his chin, swiping her thumb across his cheek.

Although narrowed to slits, he opened his eyes, absorbing the wonder and riddle of this woman.

"I don't want to pressure you or cause any more pain. If we have to go back to that deck at the winery and start over... I'll do that. For you, Nic... I will. Because I -" She swallowed hard.

"I..." she stammered.

With every attempt to speak her truth, the words seemed to catch in her throat like a lump of lead. Heavy and suffocating, it choked her ability to express the sentiment of love that occupied her heart.

The subtle shift in her demeanor colored her unease. A fiery friction crackled between them, making Nic acutely aware of Aminah's inability to express her love verbally. With every tender stroke, the constant glimmer in her pretty brown eyes echoed resoundingly in the silence.

"Trust and transparency go hand in hand, Aminah. To trust you, I need to know you, Love. *Everything*. What *is truly* Lovie's dream?"

* * *

Aminah didn't sleep a wink. Her brain and body were buzzing with thoughts of Nicolas. His vulnerability was loud, while her guard remained unyielding. The way each word trembled on the edge of his lips, so raw and unfiltered, played like a broken record repeatedly in her mind.

After Nic walked her home, Aminah rushed into her apartment, willing herself not to cry. Quickly undressing, she turned on the shower, stepping in before the water could warm. Tilting her head back, she released a vehement wail, allowing the tears to mingle with the gentle stream.

While the cascading water was soothing, Aminah knew the droplets were only a temporary cleansing for her sorrows. With her head wrapped in a towel and her weary body draped in a robe, she boiled water for chamomile tea.

Perching in the bay window, Aminah's eyes were vacant, staring blankly out of the window as the night leisurely surrendered to the first light of day. She did not stir, just remained motionless, her mind a whirlwind of conflicting emotions and stifling secrecy.

Even calls and texts from Symphony and Syncere did not persuade her to move from her station. Thoughts of her past were a tangled web of confusion, while her hope for the future was filled with the promise of a new beginning.

Sleepily, she smiled as flashes of Nicolas danced through her mind. The day they met, the nights they talked until sleep overcame them, the first time he comforted her after a nightmare—every cherished memory was a spark of joy that ignited a fire under her. Aminah hopped up from the window and rushed to her bedroom. She dressed haphazardly and stormed out of her condo.

My door is always open whenever you are ready to free yourself of all of this baggage.

"I'm ready," Aminah shouted, standing to her feet.

Dr. Jacky's eyes widened as she slowly meandered down the hallway of her office building. She surveyed Aminah's disheveled appearance, reddened eyes, and puffy cheeks. She'd been sitting on the floor leaning against the good doctor's door for at least an hour.

"Aminah… My dear. Are you alright?"

She nodded.

"You said when I was ready to free myself that I could come. I'm ready."

Dr. Jacky unlocked the door then motioned for Aminah to come in.

"Have a seat. Give me just a minute."

Aminah paced the short length of the waiting room, pausing only when the doctor's assistant, Sandra, walked through the door.

"Ms. Loveless, good morning," she said cautiously because Aminah appeared out of her mind. "Um, do you have an appointment?" Sandra asked but knew the answer.

"Good morning, Sandra. Can you please clear my morning?" Dr. Jacky said, appearing in the doorway.

Sandra nodded, darting her eyes from the doctor to the fidgety patient. Dr. Jacky nodded for Aminah to come into her office.

"Now, Ms. Aminah. Slow down and tell me what is going on."

Aminah resumed her pacing, but it was a slow, placid pace this time.

"I dreamed about Malakai. It's been weeks since any nightmares. I thought I was getting better. Escaping the ghosts. I thought I was healing." Aminah halted, turning her gaze to the doctor sitting in her chair.

"Healing is a process. And grief... Grief is a sharp ache and constant pain in the chest that refuses to be ignored. Yes, with time it softens, changes shape, but, my dear, it never goes away. It is always a silent spectator, lurking, waiting for the moment to rear its head. A relentless reminder of the endless hole left behind by those we've lost." Dr. Jacky's tone was always so powerful... strong. But in that moment, her voice trembled slightly, reminding Aminah that even the strong are weakened by grief.

"But through the heavy burdens of grief, gratefulness and gratitude can exist. Days where just a mere shimmer of sunlight can produce a smile, a heartwarming memory. Moments when you can find joy in *something or someone*, the blessings that life still has to offer." The good doctor inhaled deeply and exhaled a cleansing breath, inspiring Aminah to follow her lead.

Dr. Jacky stood and crossed the room to join Aminah at the window. They both gazed at the clouds playing hide and seek with the sun.

"With each day every wound will heal. You'll find new love who will carry the balm of compassion, patience, and understanding to mend your broken pieces. But this does not mean Malakai will be erased. I am confident that you'll always have room for him in your heart."

Silence wafted through the air like a comforting breeze, lifting her spirits second by second. Aminah blinked, permitting the tears to flow. Smiling, she looked at the good doctor, appreciative for her liberating declaration.

"I'm ready," Aminah rasped.

With just those few words, the burden of her unspoken truths loosened their grip as she prepared to lay bare her soul.

"Ready for what, my dear?"

"To tell the truth."

Dr. Jacky nodded, patiently waiting to listen whenever Aminah was ready to speak. They dallied for what felt like eternity, but the waiting wasn't discomforting. Clearing away the flood of tears with the back of her hand, Aminah blew out a breath. Absently staring out of the window, she uttered.

"Malakai isn't a ghost. He's not dead."

13

"Lovie. What are you doing here?" Nic said, standing in the threshold of his loft's door.

"Can you take me somewhere? Please," Aminah pled, her eyes blood-shot red.

Angst immediately cloaked him. Nic nodded, rushing to put on a shirt and shoes as she lingered in the doorway. They walked in silence to his car. He scanned her for a moment. Aminah was dressed in joggers with a wrinkled denim shirt. Her short curls were pushed back with a headband. Glasses rest on top of her reddened nose.

Nic had so many questions but his lovie was stoic and zombiesque. He opened her door, before quickly rounding the car to get in.

"Where to?"

"7900 Crescent Boulevard."

Nic had driven for almost an hour when he pulled up to a security gate. The guard approached the vehicle and asked for identification. Aminah leaned over the console, extending her arm to give the guard her information.

"Two guests," the man spoke through the walkie-talkie attached to his sleeve.

Still hushed, Aminah directed him where to park with pointed fingers and hand gestures. She exited the car, not waiting for him to open her door as usual.

"They'll check you for sharp objects," she finally said.

Nic nodded.

"Aminah. What is this place?" His furrowed brow displayed confusion and caution.

"Just trust me. This one time," she pleaded.

Walking through the double doors of the building, they were stripped of their keys and phones and placed in a locker. Nic and Aminah were escorted into a room and waited for roughly fifteen minutes. He pressed a gentle hand to her right leg, which bounced uncontrollably. Her wriggling ceased as she peered into his worried, pleading eyes. He wanted answers, and it was finally time that she entrusted him with her truth.

"Aminah," a soft voice hailed from the doorway.

A brown skinned older woman with salt and pepper hair pulled back into a ponytail smiled sweetly.

"Mrs. Bradley. Hello," Aminah said, standing from her chair to greet the woman.

"Hello. It's good to see you," Mrs. Bradley volleyed, pulling her into a hug.

"You brought company. Who is this handsome gentleman?"

Nic stood, extended his hand to shake hers.

"This is my friend, Nic. Nicolas Touissant."

"Nice to meet you, Nic," Mrs. Bradley said.

The earnest smile still painted her face.

While he was thinking, *What the fuck is going on?* - he uttered, "Hello. Nice to meet you as well."

"Are we ready?" Mrs. Bradley asked.

Nic's eyes danced back and forth confusedly. Aminah linked her hand in his, squeezing three times to calm his concerns. He accompanied Mrs. Bradley and Aminah down a bright green hallway.

"Here we go," Mrs. Bradley announced. "I'll give you a moment."

She took a few steps back and leaned against the wall to give them privacy.

Aminah stared through a large picture window, and Nic's eyes followed. The small room was bare except for a table, chair, wooden easel, canvas boards, and paint. Anyone who walked down the hallway could not help but stop and admire the magnificent mural that decorated the walls.

Nic's eyes widened. Aminah's likeness was embedded in a kaleidoscope of colors captured so vividly. So beautiful. He shifted to look at her. She smiled but never disconnected her gaze from the figure in the room.

"Nicolas Touissant, meet Malakai Winston," she faintly introduced.

Nic blinked rapidly, stunned to realize that the *ghost* he had called Malakai was, in fact, not a ghost at all. He was a living, breathing man whose appearance was not as stately as Nic had seen in pictures.

"Months before I met you, Malakai had a mental break and tried to kill himself," Aminah announced.

"For months before that, he started to change. Became distant, paranoid, wouldn't sleep for days. Then... the dark days. It was like someone flipped a switch and never flipped it back." She shrugged, eyes trained on a detached version of Malakai.

"Kai started hallucinating. Always anxious and confused. Suspicious of everyone... *including me.* He would get so mad that I started just staying away as much as I could. But that day was actually a good day. We cooked dinner, watched a movie... and then... *flick,"* she said, motioning her finger as if turning off a light switch.

"I'd been afraid of his outburst before but that time..." She shook her head. "... That time I thought I was going to die." Aminah's voice cracked as tears poured from her eyes.

"He had a knife. And that's all I ever see in my dreams," she cried, fingering the scar on her chin.

"I think he left because he didn't want to hurt me. But he shouldn't have gotten into the car. He shouldn't -" her word faltered.

Nic wrapped her in his arms, stroking his hands through her hair.

Whimpering, he muttered, "Lovie, it's okay. It's okay. Shh. You're okay, Love."

Aminah wailed for several tragic heartbeats. Clearing her throat, she wiped her eyes then lifted from Nic's warm embrace.

"He crashed into a tree less than a mile from our house. He was spiraling while I was soaring and I didn't even know. I wouldn't let myself see the truth. So when he woke up, he made me promise to always take care of him... to always *love* him. It was the least that I could do."

Nic felt like he'd been hit by a ton of bricks. Her admittance of the secrets she'd been carrying was the missing piece of the puzzle. She stared up at Nicolas and without a word spoken, she sought solace in him... understanding.

"When I met you, Nic, I thought, '*how could the universe be so cruel?*' You were perfect. You *are* perfect. But I made a promise. But then I fell in love with you. And instead of facing my demons, I ran. Finding safety in solitude rather than being vulnerable to opening my heart again."

Unable to find the right remarks at the moment, he kissed her forehead, nose, and lips. Swiping the loose tendrils from her brow, he stared at this beautifully shattered woman that he was ready, willing, and able to protect and mend every broken piece.

"I love you," he whispered, uttering the only words he was certain of.

Nic simply stared at her, regarding every speckle of brown in her pretty eyes, the plumpness of her pouty lips, and every iota of love reflected in her stare.

"Aminah. Are you ready?" Mrs. Bradley checked, resting a gentle hand on her shoulder.

He silently conveyed his love with a gentle touch and a lingering gaze. His fingertips lingered against her skin. Nic didn't want to let her go but understood that she needed to say farewell.

Entering the room, Aminah admired each meticulous brushstroke painted with a tender caress. The mural stretched across the walls like a love letter written by a rainbow. Her eyes fluttered over the story of their shared journey. Thankfully, this masterpiece did not reflect the tragic end.

"Mr. Winston, you have a visitor," Mrs. Bradley said softly.

He slowly spun around. Aminah smiled, admiring his face as she shed a tear. Malakai was still the most beautiful man she'd ever seen. His locs had grown since the last time she was there, but his sister always kept them groomed. His shirt and joggers were stained with paint, which was a good sign. Painting meant Malakai was having a good day.

"Do you know who this is?" Mrs. Bradley asked.

He nodded.

"Who?" she probed further.

"Peanut," he whispered.

"I painted you today." Malakai continued.

"You did? Can I see?"

Although her hands were trembling, Aminah was not afraid of him anymore.

He nodded and raised his chin towards the canvas resting on the easel. She pulled back the white draping. Her breath hitched. It was an image of them swinging on the hammock in his backyard the night he first said, '*I love you*.'

Aminah released a gut wrenching cry.

"I'm so sorry, Kai. I'm so sorry."

She didn't realize that he'd walked towards her. Malakai slid his hands across her waist, resting his chin on her shoulder.

He began to sing, "Malakai and Minah, sitting in a tree, k-i-s-s-i-n-g."

Aminah chuckled through her sobs.

Thumbing away her tears, he focused on her eyes and declared, "It's okay, Peanut. I'm okay."

That simple declaration was the emancipation she needed to be set free. Malakai released her hand and returned to his paint station. A silent understanding passed between them.

Aminah turned to walk away when her eyes connected with Nic's. A newfound sense of lightness sparkled in her dewy eyes. While she would always cherish the memories of the past, she felt a sense of closure wash over her.

Rushing into Nic's arms was like embarking on a new horizon. Like a blank canvas ready for her to paint a picture of fresh promises and new love.

14

Nic opened the door to his condo and stepped aside to allow Aminah to walk in. She slipped off her shoes while he hung her jacket in the closet. Heavy lidded eyes stared at him as if she needed permission to move.

Aminah was exhausted and maybe a bit delirious after an emotionally charged day. She fell asleep as soon as her head hit the rest in the car. When he asked where she wanted to go and what she needed, her only answer was, *"Home... with you."*

Surveying his condo, she noticed several significant changes since the last time she'd visited. New furniture filled the once empty space, family portraits and personal artifacts minimized the industrial feel. The card table in the dining room was gone, replaced with a gorgeous vintage piece that she guessed came from his house in Brighton Falls.

Advancing further into the great room, she slowly perused and suddenly halted her prance. Aminah's eyes wandered up the lengthy soft gray walls decorated with two massive, familiar paintings. Her eyes misted in recognition of the riot of colors and textures outlining the breathtaking landscape. *From the Collection of Malakai Ford.* She silently read the inscription.

Twisting around to face him she uttered, "Nic." Shock and appreciation laced her face.

"You said the place needed work, so I took your recommendations and decorated it a little," he said, shrugging.

"The paintings," she mumbled, unable to comprehend this miracle masquerading as a regular man.

"I remember you showing these to me. I bought them for you... but then you..." his voice waned.

Aminah nodded her understanding. He purchased the paintings for her but she left.

Her throat suddenly dried as she croaked, "They're beautiful. You... Nic... You're beautiful."

Aminah closed the distance between them with a sense of urgency. As he began to form words on his lips in response, she pressed her lips against his, rendering him speechless with a firm, yet tender kiss. She hoped that her touch silenced his doubts and fears. Deepening the kiss, they became lost in the quiet intimacy of the warm embrace.

"Lovie," he growled. "You need some food, baby. Rest," he stuttered, unsuccessfully attempting to reason with her.

Delicate hands roaming across his chest made it almost impossible for him to complete his sentence.

"Shh," Aminah hissed, dragging two fingers over his puffy lips. "I said I don't want or need anything but you, Nicolas Avery Touissant."

Clutching the curves of his chiseled face, she licked the seam of his lips, sliding her thick tongue in his mouth. Aminah kissed him tranquilly, tenderly, opening her eyes to ensure he was still in the moment. And he was.

That kiss consumed Nic. Lost in her beautiful eyes. He wanted to experience every corner and crevice of her pussy right then and there, but once again, he was following her lead. Clasping her waist, he lifted her, positioning her legs to straddle him.

They stood connected in the middle of the floor. Nic's hands traversed up and down her body, holding her so close she was becoming like a second layer of skin. Aminah passionately tangled her thick thighs around his waist as she trailed kisses down his neck then nestled there for an extended heartbeat.

Nic spun around gently settling them on the couch. His fingertips crawled under her shirt, caressing her warm flesh.

"Shit, Love."

Nic's eyes rolled to the back of his head as he slowly laid back on the couch with Aminah still attached. Unhooking her bra, he stripped her bare in one swift move. Sweet kisses lingered over plump, perky breasts. Her body was a masterpiece. Every curve and contour held a testimony.

"You are fucking perfection," he moaned, slipping and sliding his tongue over her taut nipples.

Her heart raced with salacious anticipation. Energy coursed through her veins in the sheer bliss of their reunion. But this time, Aminah was truly free. Liberated from the secrets that held her captive. At last, his kiss, warm caress, and unmatched adoration held the promise of another day. *Maybe even a lifetime.*

With every lick, nip, and touch, Aminah counted down the minutes until his weighty life source penetrated her sodden essence.

"Mmmm, Nic, please," Aminah whined, *shit,* begged.

"Be patient, Love. Do we have a reason to rush or can I take my time?"

Pouting, she nodded. Nic snickered.

Tracing his thumb across the band of her pants, Nic nudged her pants down. Never relinquishing from the sweltering kiss, he smacked and squeezed her thong-cladded ass to the rhythm of their tongue lashing.

He wasn't bullshitting about taking his time. Their foreplay was a slow burn, a delicate dance that left them both gasping for breath. Nic was familiar with every arc, dent and dip of her naked body. But the first time they made love, she wasn't completely bare because his Aminah was laden with unreasonable obligation. But *his lovie* was finally *his* - unburdened, cleared from all previous commitment.

Unapologetically, he ogled her. Gazed watchfully because her beauty was more than skin deep. Every scar, stitch of pain, and flood of grief bejeweled her crown and she wore it like a badge of honor.

Aminah radiated from within, illuminating every inch of her flawless skin and Nic was hypnotized. Swiping his knuckle down her face, he smiled sexily and she returned the gesture. Nic trailed a finger down her neck, between her breasts, over her stomach, and landed on his final destination, her clit.

Intoxicating heat shot through her body. Every nerve ending fired like a rocket as she sucked in a breath. The gradual escalation of desire was going to be her undoing. Aminah was ready to surrender, throw in the damn towel.

"Please. Bae. Please," she crooned.

Smirking, he slid pearly white teeth over his bottom. Nic fisted the back of her head and pulled her down so that they were face-to-face.

"Come here, Love."

"Where?" she purred.

"Up here."

Nic pointed to his mouth.

Aminah's hickory orbs grew wide. Being a girl who always followed the rules worked in her favor in this instance. Slowly... carefully, she scaled the length of his body, maneuvering her thickness with the grace of a ballerina.

In the esteemed words of our one and only First Lady Michelle Obama, "when they go low, you go high." And that's exactly what they did. As he descended down her body, she ascended up his, co-facilitating a lascivious excursion.

Dipping his tongue into the grooves of her navel, he halted, preparing himself to be re-introduced to her velvety smooth dripping folds. If his memory served him correctly, her pussy was pretty and plush and pouring.

Fondling her chocolate areolas, she gradually reached the top of the mountain. Her bodacious thighs pleasantly smothered him, fat ass settled against his chest. Nic closed his eyes, relishing in the sugary aroma of her treasure. His eyes traced up the arc of her glorious body. They gazed deeply at one another - her, soliciting safety, and him, seeking permission.

"Your pussy is dripping baby. Can I clean that up?" Nic sexily licked his lips.

Aminah nodded.

"Please. And don't miss a drop."

Nic enjoyed this version of his lovie. Carefree, sensual, and nasty.

Deeply inhaling, he delighted in her delectable fragrance, which was reminiscent of the winery's bakery—sugar and spice and everything nice.

Nic kissed her private lips - faintly, delicately, passionately. Aminah's eyes rolled as she lost all control of her limbs. She mounted his handsome face with the perfect dancer's arc in her back as she tightly gripped the arm of the couch.

Even the softness of his touch was too aggressive for her sensitivity. It had been too long, and *he* was simply too much. The air was cool yet thick, but it was him who snatched her breath away. Her oxygen supply momentarily denied.

"Nic, shh - shh - shh."

Nic released a moan of his own because she tasted exactly like he'd imagined - *heavenly*. Slurping to the rhythm of their passion-filled cries, the delightful taste of her essence gratified his gluttony. Aminah was his vice - the only thing he wanted in excess. He was greedy and she fed him every ounce of her pussy.

Grinding her curvy hips, riding every stroke of his tongue against her clit. Nic kneaded and squeezed her plump ass while plunging into her sodden hole - supping, sucking, nibbling, withdrawing her surplus.

"Nic. Oh shit. Oh shit. Bae, I'm coming."

"Mm-hmm." He moaned in agreement.

"Nicolas! Fuck!"

Aminah quivered, teeth chattered as he emptied her. She was bankrupt, completely drained. Labored, ragged breathing, Aminah dropped her head, staring at Nic still resting between her legs. She was immobile, legs still quivering through the aftershock.

"Come here, Love," he uttered, while simultaneously lifting her weakened body from his face.

Aminah layed next to him, caressing that robust python lounging on his stomach. One soft stroke, then another, and Nic became undone. Turning her to the side with her ass cradled against him, he lifted her leg to drape across his. Steadily, he slipped inside of her ocean but paused to revel in the moment. Sensually, they kissed and licked and petted, communicating a thousand words without ever speaking.

His fingertips traced patterns of love and longing across her skin. This was all consuming. Every touch setting him ablaze like a wildfire. It had been too long.

"I missed the fuck out of you, Aminah. Don't leave again," he whispered, hope and hurt broke his tenor.

"I won't. I promise, Nic. I'm yours," Aminah cried.

Repositioning her leg, she arched her back, forcing him to deeply penetrate her center. She missed him, but she craved that dick. It was like a drug, intoxicating and addictive, and Aminah feigned the potent rush of pleasure with each calculated stroke.

"Lovie," Nic moaned.

"Nic," Aminah rasped.

"Baby," he hissed.

"Damn," she groaned.

With each whispered word, their lovemaking built to a tantalizing crescendo. Their bodies laid limp and ablaze with desire.

Hours later, Nic and Aminah finally made it to his bed after their bodies tangled in a passionate choreographed dance. Foreheads connected, they lay wide awake, resting in each other's tranquility. Nic's eyes were closed, but he wasn't sleeping. Mutedly, she traced the curves of his face, the bulge of his Adam's apple, and the contour of his chest. Nic was constructed with divine craftsmanship.

"What happens now?" Aminah mumbled breathily.

Nic lazily lifted his eyes.

"You stay. We date. We love," he said then paused as he fingered her lips.

"I move your shit to my place and then give you forever," Nic snickered but he was serious.

Aminah giggled, kissing against his fingers.

"So what happens now, Love?" he asked, copying her question to him.

"I stay. We date. We love. I move my shit in and then give you forever. I love you, Nic."

His lips curved into a gentle, forgiving smile—a quiet yet powerful promise that the wounds of yesterday were gone and the healing of tomorrow began.

"I love you, *Love*."

EPILOGUE

"Lovie, we're going to be late," Nic said, his voice echoing into the bedroom.

Aminah walked down the hallway, securing her earring before she said, "You could've left without me, honey. The party *is* happening right downstairs."

Nic smiled, overjoyed every time she effortlessly uttered his new moniker... *honey.*

"Damn, love. It was worth the wait."

He winked before roaming his eyes over the shiny gold spaghetti-strap dress hanging above her knees. Aminah's skin was still sun-kissed from their weekend getaway in Napa Valley.

Six months had speedily ticked by, and the newly minted couple hadn't stopped to take a breath. After learning about Malachai, Nic needed some time to process. Mutually agreeing, they dated before considering *moving her shit in.*

Dating only lasted *maybe* three months before Nic and Aminah were lugging her boxes down Main Street to his loft. He entirely remodeled his place, adding walls to make an office and space for her art collection. Artistic touches influenced by Aminah were everywhere, and he loved them.

Nic had even encouraged her to continue seeing Dr. Jacky and visit Malakai regularly. She decided to only go on special occasions like his birthday and Christmas, but she was thankful that Nic would accompany her each time.

"You look beautiful, baby," Nic said, closing the distance between them.

Kissing her forehead, he pulled her into a taut hug, grabbing two handfuls of ass. Aminah giggled, playfully pushing him away.

"Bae, stop," she sang, then sank deeper into his embrace.

Hand in hand, they strolled out of their home and down the flight of steps to enter the back door of Grapes and Mash. Tonight was the official grand opening. Nic hosted small parties and private events to test new products but postponed the official opening until he felt everything was perfect.

When he entered the bar, his sister Naomi was the first to greet him, followed by her boyfriend Amir and then his mother. As usual, Naomi prepared all the dishes. The delectable aromas wafting through the space made Nic and Aminah's stomachs rumble.

"Hey Nicky. This place looks great," she squealed, hugging him tightly.

"Thanks, Nomi. It smells great," he teased.

"Mom. I'm glad you could come," Nic announced, securing his other arm around his mother.

"I wouldn't miss it. Your dad would be proud. He *is* proud," she said, wiping a stray tear from her face. He stared at the painting of his father on the wall.

It wasn't often that Aminah was the creator of art instead of the teacher of it. But one evening, shortly after she moved in, she helped Nic close up after an event and surprised him with the very first and likely the only Aminah Loveless painting.

The image of his father leaning against a fence overlooking the winery's grounds while the sun shone over him was so vivid and real that Nic immediately cried. That night, he hung it above the Grapes and Mash sign over the bar for every patron to admire.

"Yeah. I think he's proud too," Nic finally spoke.

The Touissant family was silent as they gazed at the painting.

"Aminah, you look beautiful," Mrs. Touissant said, breaking the muteness.

"Thank you. You look gorgeous as always," Aminah declared, kissing his mother on the cheek.

"And Ms. Nomi, you are a brickhouse girl," Aminah cooed, admiring Naomi's thickness in the skin-tight dress.

Aminah and Naomi settled their differences after their previous unpleasant encounter. Naomi only wanted happiness for her brother, and Aminah was that for him. As long as Aminah treated her Nicky right, Naomi was happy to have a new sister-friend.

The crowd grew as the night persisted. Family, friends, and business associates enjoyed delicious food, wine, and bourbon as they mingled with jazz and R&B music curling the air. Aminah's parents even joined in on the festivities.

Nic's eyes danced around the room, digesting the thrill of the night. The best part; the crew was finally mended, but with a slight change of course. Instead of being *the friends* among married couples, Nic and Aminah were together as friends *and* lovers. The third link in the couples' trio was complete.

"So Nic, I bet you five hundred dollars that a winter wonderland wedding at the winery is in your future," King teased, remembering when Nic made the same bet about him and Syncere's future.

"Shiid, knowing this nigga, he ain't waiting for the winter to make Aminah *Mrs. Touissant,*" Tyus joked.

But the expression on Nic's face stopped both of them in their tracks.

"Dawg, you good?" King asked.

Nic nodded, then walked away. Approaching the DJ booth, he motioned for the microphone. The music faded before he spoke.

"Good evening. Good evening, everyone," Nic announced, quieting the partygoers.

"Thank you all for coming out tonight. It's been a long time coming. I'm thankful to see the dream in my head come to life. I put my blood, sweat, and tears in every fiber of this place, and I appreciate every one of you who has supported me."

Nic paused to receive claps and well-wishes from his friends and family before he continued.

"My mom and dad always encouraged me and my sister to follow our dreams. To never allow yourself to get too comfortable. After my dad died, I lost sight of his words for a bit. I became too comfortable and lost confidence in my ability to dream because I was too afraid to fail," he said, eyes blankly gazing over the crowd.

"But a very special friend of mine reminded me that failing makes the success that much greater. *You'll never fail until you try,*" Nic chuckled, mimicking Aminah's voice.

Shifting his eyes towards *her*, he smiled.

"She manifested that this would happen for me," he said, circling his finger around the space. "And I am forever grateful."

Aminah's pretty brown eyes filled with unshed tears. With her hands clasped together and nestled under her chin, she stared at him with so much love, respect, and pride.

"So... to honor my father, I am going to continue to go after my dreams," he exclaimed, stepping down from the platform with the mic still in hand.

"Aminah, my love. I have loved you since the day my eyes connected with yours. You are the smartest, wittiest, goofiest..." he chuckled. "...Most beautiful woman I've ever encountered."

Her breath caught in her throat as shock and disbelief washed over her.

What is he doing? Is he really doing this?

"Lovie, from the moment I met you, my life has been filled with joy and purpose. You have been my spades partner, pool shark, and drinking buddy." They simultaneously laughed, reminiscing about the fun they'd shared.

"You are the carrier of my secrets, my confidante, and my best damn friend. I tried to imagine my life without you but the shit is impossible because you are the sun. Even when I tried to hide, you shined on my darkest days. So..." Nic's voice faltered as he kneeled on one knee.

Reaching into his jacket pocket, he fumbled with the blue box and the microphone. King quickly trotted to his friend. Grabbing the mic, he held it to Nic's mouth. Slowly, Nic opened the box to reveal a sparkling brilliant diamond.

Aminah gasped; the tears previously trapped in the corners of her eyes freed.

"So, just like you believed in me, I believe in us. I want to share our dreams, fears, and joys... together. I want you, Aminah Rae Loveless. I want us... forever. Can I make you Mrs. Touissant, love?"

In the sudden stillness of the room, the pounding in her chest was the only sound. Aminah roughly swallowed; a rush of fear and *forever* flooded her system as she fought to breathe. Flashes overwhelmed her mind: Nic, the day they first met, walks in the park, and the nights they made love.

With family and friends gathered on pins and needles, she cupped his face, while a toothless smile adorned hers.

Aminah stood before him free from ghosts and all skeletons unearthed. With a steady and unwavering voice she said, "I want you, Nicolas Avery Touissant. I want us... forever. Yes, honey, it would be my honor to be your wife."

The onlookers exhaled, roaring in cheers and tears as the DJ blasted Mary J. Blige's "Share My World."

Sharing a tender, lingering kiss, Nic and Aminah did not hear a sound. Consumed in their bond, the world around them hushed. Their hearts beat as one in a symphonic melody of love, forgiveness, commitment, and pure joy.

"Thank you, babe," Aminah whispered.

"For what, baby," Nic asked, resting his lips against her temple.

"For loving me unconditionally... soul, heart and mind."

THE END

HEY LOVE!

Learn more about the Robbi Renee Collection

www.robbirenee.com

www.ingramcontent.com/pod-product-compliance
Lightning Source LLC
LaVergne TN
LVHW020046110826
845155LV00029B/641

* 9 7 8 1 9 5 4 7 6 7 5 0 8 *